THE FOUR-WAY SPLIT

An innocent man accused of robbery and murder travels from Redrock, Arizona to the Yuma state penitentiary by stage. Suddenly, John Flint D'Arragon breaks away from Marshal Mick Imlach. He takes Fran Parker as hostage and, in a desperate race across the desert, is pursued by lawmen, Fran's father and the violent Pike Rickman. D'Arragon is drawn to the waters of the San Pedro where, in a blazing six-gun climax, he must face the outlaw Rickman and gain his freedom.

MATT LAIDLAW

THE FOUR-WAY SPLIT

Complete and Unabridged

LINFORD
Leicester

First published in Great Britain in 2005 by
Robert Hale Limited
London

First Linford Edition
published 2006
by arrangement with
Robert Hale Limited
London

British Library CIP Data

Laidlaw, Matt
    The four-way split.—Large print ed.—
Linford western library
1. Western stories
2. Large type books
I. Title
813.5'4 [F]

ISBN 1–84617–243–8

Published by
F. A. Thorpe (Publishing)
Anstey, Leicestershire

Set by Words & Graphics Ltd.
Anstey, Leicestershire
Printed and bound in Great Britain by
T. J. International Ltd., Padstow, Cornwall

This book is printed on acid-free paper

PART ONE

PART ONE

Prologue

'The way I see it,' the stranger said, 'your bank's ripe and ready for the picking.'

'And you know about that from experience?' the saloonist said. He was wiping a glass with a rag grey with dirt. His eyes were blank; every so often he pushed out his lower lip and chewed at the ragged ends of his bushy black moustache.

'Some.'

'Which side?'

'Which side what?'

'This experience of banks. Did you come by it from bein' inside or outside the law?'

'Ah,' the stranger said. 'Now *you're* stepping outside the bounds of good taste. All I'm doing is trying to help the people of Redrock keep hold of their money.'

'So shouldn't you be advising the marshal? Or the man who runs the bank?'

'They here? If so, I'll be happy to oblige.'

'Nope. But the jail office is down the street.'

'Maybe tomorrow.'

'My guess is tomorrow you won't be here.'

'I'm heading for the San Pedro — maybe I'll stay in Redrock tonight, maybe not . . .'

The stranger shrugged. He was alone at the bar, sipping tepid beer, soaking up the warmth of the setting sun that was low enough to send its rays slanting in through the saloon's windows. His remarks were well intentioned. He'd ridden into town — passing through on his way east towards the San Pedro River and then on to Texas — and observed the position of the bank, the naked, defenceless windows to the rear over-looking a maze of alleys leading to the town's outskirts, the distance from the bank's front doors to the marshal's office which was situated around a bend in the street and out of sight.

He'd been making idle conversation on a warm evening with the smell of sawdust and coal oil and cheap alcohol in his nostrils, whiling away an hour or so in the almost empty saloon before riding off into the dusk. The subject he'd raised was of major importance to Redrock's citizens, of only passing interest to the stranger if his observations fell on deaf ears. He forgot about it, turned to drink his beer facing the bright windows with his elbows hooked on the bar, his last thought being idle speculation that maybe he'd opened his mouth and in doing so made a big mistake.

If he could have read the saloonist's thoughts, he would have been more concerned. As he rattled glasses and generally kept himself occupied until his establishment began to fill up, the big man — who was also a member of the town council — was trying to figure out who the stranger was, and what the hell he was playing at.

Could be he was testing the water: an official of some kind about to jump on Amos Grant, the owner of the bank: a federal man in town to check on the marshal? Or maybe he was an outlaw, so amazed at what he saw as the Redrock bank's vulnerability he couldn't keep it to himself.

Well, the saloonist thought, tomorrow was another day. He'd talk to Marshal Imlach, drop the stranger's interesting notions in the lawman's lap and step back out of the way. It would come to something or nothing but, either way, long experience had taught the saloonist always to look after number one by covering his back.

But the stranger was oblivious. He listened absently to the clink of glasses, nodded occasionally as the swing doors flapped and thirsty men in dusty working clothes came through to step up to the bar, thought again about booking in for the night at the hotel or pushing on — and finally settled on the latter.

He turned, placed his empty glass, sent a coin ringing on the bar. Then he was out in the street where a cool evening breeze was being sucked in by the rising heat, in the saddle and swinging away from the rail — and all the while he was conscious of eyes watching his departure, and of the nagging conviction that he'd opened his mouth once too often.

1

Marshal Mick Imlach was convinced of one thing: if John Flint D'Arragon could escape, he would.

For every yard of every hot, dusty mile the Hatch & Hodges Concord rattled and lurched across Arizona Territory, D'Arragon would be scheming, his keen eyes probing the other passengers for opportunity, his escort for the one chink in his armour that would offer him hope. At every likely ambush site those same desperate eyes would turn to the Concord's narrow windows with their flapping leather curtains and search the arid hills for the flash of sunlight on a gun barrel, his ears attuned for the crack of a gunshot that would signal a daring attempt at rescue, his muscles tensed to deliver the violent blow opening the way to a reckless leap to freedom.

Oh yes, if the slimmest of opportunities presented itself then this tall, lean man with the haggard face and hungry eyes would snatch at it, and make his break. And, as they had done through the past twenty hours and several station stops for fresh teams, those warning thoughts hammered at Marshal Mick Imlach's brain. They helped keep him awake, and alert, just as the awareness of the steel manacle clamped to his wrist and the chain links that tethered him to the prisoner afforded some reassurance. Every movement, by either man, was transmitted through those steel links and drew a furtive sidelong glance. In his swift, burning glances, D'Arragon managed to convey amusement, and contempt, and that contempt came from the knowledge that the marshal could also see in his sunken eyes the tremendous reserves of energy and willpower that would always refuse to admit defeat. In his turn, Imlach strove to leave his eyes empty of feeling, to convey indifference that suggested supreme confidence, to suggest energy-sapping boredom at being forced to carry out the routine task of escorting a convicted murderer to life imprisonment in Yuma.

John Flint D'Arragon would escape, Imlach thought with unnerving conviction: one way or another, the man a local blacksmith had manacled to his wrist would make the attempt; he would do so before the Concord rattled into Yuma; and he would do so because he was facing a lifetime behind bars in the state penitentiary for a crime he insisted had been committed by another man.

And what worried Marshal Mick Imlach more than anything was that, with Yuma now agonizingly close, he didn't know how long he'd be able to stay awake.

2

There was patience within him. That patience bred and nurtured an unnatural and unnerving watchfulness, and with that watchfulness, inevitably, there came hope.

Belief in the inevitability of hope — if a man was blessed with the patience to wait long enough — was a trait that had seen the relentless, indefatigable John Flint D'Arragon emerge unscathed from countless clashes with violent men on the West's lawless frontiers; clashes in which he had frequently been branded as guilty because hair-raising escapes ahead of enraged citizens, after a killing done in self-defence, left nobody in those desert towns to argue in his favour.

And so it was ironic but not unexpected when an encounter and the ensuing murder that had put him on the long trail to life in the Yuma state pen had been between other men, in another place, at a time when Flint D'Arragon was sleeping rough in scrub on the banks of the San Pedro River.

Sleeping rough, and alone. No witnesses. But there had been several witnesses who had placed him forty miles west of his lonely bed beneath the stars, at the scene of a bank robbery and murder; several who had insisted they had been in the bank to see him pull the trigger of the Greener that had almost ripped Amos Grant's head from his shoulders. And it had been those witnesses who had pointed Marshal Mick Imlach in the right direction, told him the best time to catch D'Arragon with his pants and his guard down, then prowled like circling coyotes — but at a safe distance — when the lawman moved in for the kill.

For willing, law-abiding witnesses, D'Arragon mused, read outlaws, enemies — and liars and, as he wondered yet again whose path he had

13

crossed one time too many, which gunfighter's pride he had wounded, whose reputation he had sullied — and let the bitterness and frustration show in his narrowed eyes and in the clenched muscles of his jaw — he sensed someone watching him and lifted his head quickly to look across the coach and meet the clear blue eyes of the young woman.

The Concord clattered and lurched. Up above, the driver snarled a curse at his sweating, six-horse team. Pink suffused the slim young woman's cheeks as she allowed the coach's fierce swaying to rock her sideways so that her dark hair swept across her face and broke their locked gaze. But the motion also threw her awkwardly against the businessman sitting next to her. Instinctively, as most men would, he grinned with pleasure — then suddenly shot an apprehensive glance at D'Arragon when the woman winced and twisted away as her hip pressed hard against his.

Six-gun, D'Arragon decided, carried

high on the right hip under the man's black frock coat, and it had hurt her — and suddenly hope flared. If he was right, it was the only weapon in the Concord's cramped and dusty interior: before allowing anybody to board the coach, Imlach had ensured that the four men and one woman were unarmed. He had also made a great show of unbuckling his own gunbelt and handing it to the driver; for a lawman on escort duty, allowing the butt of a six-gun to jut invitingly between him and his prisoner would have been a bad mistake.

Yet, as careful as he had been, one man's deviousness threatened to wreck all his good work. D'Arragon had heard the burly, black-clad cattleman object to being disarmed, and now realized the man had somehow kept the pistol away from the marshal's searching hands. Maybe he was expecting trouble; Geronimo and his Chiricahua braves were restless and, against those odds, one man riding shotgun was the stage company's token show of strength and did little to reassure passengers. But whatever the man's fears or reasons for stubbornly clinging to his weapon, now, almost certainly without Imlach's knowledge, D'Arragon had been thrown a lifeline.

Though it was late afternoon the heat was a solid weight beating down on the swaying coach, turning the interior into a Dutch oven where grey dust drifted like gritty mist. D'Arragon was tight up against the window. Imlach was at his left shoulder, a fat drummer and an unshaven cowboy stinking of whiskey on the marshal's left. The centre bench was empty. Across it, opposite D'Arragon, another drummer, small, light of build and wearing a cotton suit, was lazily looking out over the barren, sun-baked terrain as the leather curtains flapped in the hot breeze. Next to him was the big cattleman in the black frock coat, and the girl, dark and strikingly beautiful in a gingham frock, was tight against that man's right side

— and the pistol.

Somehow that pistol, lethal currency more valuable than gold dust because it would buy him freedom, had to be brought within reach of D'Arragon's eager hands. And — even as an idea came flashing into his mind — with a soft, nasal snort, Marshal Mick Imlach lost his fight to stay awake, closed his eyes and drifted into an uneasy doze.

D'Arragon's mouth went dry. Before his eyes, the door to freedom was creaking open. His pulse was like the insistent beat of a distant drum in his ears, the urge to spring into immediate action almost irresistible.

Since boarding the Concord, D'Arragon had evolved no plan. Hazily, as the miles rattled by, he had thought about the need for a horse to put distance between him and the inevitable posse, a weapon to make a stand if he was cornered. But he had come on to the coach as a prisoner manacled to a hard-headed, cold-eyed lawman, the heavy chain was an unbreakable link between them, so thoughts had been idle daydreams, a way of passing time while he awaited the dawn of hope. But now . . .

As Imlach again snorted softly and slipped sideways to lean against the fat drummer, D'Arragon casually reached out, pulled the leather curtain to one side. The sinking sun was almost due west and he said, quietly, as if to himself, 'Oh, my God — Apaches.'

That one muttered word, Apache, was the match that lit the tinder-dry undergrowth, the dazzling flash of lightning that sent the lead steer crazy with fear and stampeded the herd. The man in black came out of his seat in a bull-like lunge. The girl uttered a grunt of pain as his swinging elbow drove hard into her shoulder. He half fell across the lightly built drummer, crushing the startled man back into his seat, one hand flapping wildly for the curtain. And, as he fell forward, his face thrust towards the window, his eyes wild and searching, his other hand was flipping back his coat tails and exposing the tooled leather holster and gleaming Colt .45.

D'Arragon hit him. He leaned across the centre bench and put the full weight of his muscular shoulder behind a hard left that cracked like a pistol shot against the big cattleman's jaw and dumped him in the lean drummer's lap. The dazed man sat down hard. The back of his head slammed into the little drummer's nose with a grisly crunch. In a move too fast to follow, D'Arragon shot out a hand and plucked the exposed .45 from its holster. In the same, sweeping movement, he whipped his hand around in a wide loop that slammed the pistol barrel across the sleeping marshal's skull.

Suddenly, the narrow confines of the rocking cabin seemed to be awash with blood. It gushed from the drummer's nose, turned his soft white hands into crimson gloves, spattered his suit and the leather seat. Imlach's scalp had split, and the sheen of blood was bright in his greying hair and on his face, rapidly soaking his shirt collar.

But in the seconds that had elapsed, and continued to pass with frightening speed, D'Arragon had no time to register emotion. The little drummer was cursing and breathing wetly as he struggled to heave off the heavy cattleman. The young woman raised a hand as if to ward off the horror, straining away from the droplets of sprayed blood. The cruel pistol-whipping had driven Imlach from restless doze to deep unconsciousness, and his full weight slumped on the other, sweating drummer whose eyes now bulged with terror. The unshaven cowboy sat in the corner and watched with hooded eyes and mild amusement.

In the chaos, D'Arragon jerked his arm away from Imlach so that the heavy chain imprisoning both their wrists was flat on the seat. Then he thrust the muzzle of the .45 hard against one of the links, and squeezed the trigger.

The young woman bit back a scream.

From above, a voice yelled, 'What the hell's goin' on in there?' and there was a screech and a juddering as the driver, Tom Gaines, slammed his boot on the brake.

The coach stank of cordite. D'Arragon's ears rang from the crash of the explosion. He shook his head, lifted his freed hand and sprang from his seat. With the severed chain clinking as it swung loose, he grabbed the big cattleman by the coat front, heaved him off the drummer and dumped him on the floor by the drunken cowboy.

The coach jerked, began to grind to a halt. D'Arragon was thrown forward across the centre bench. He saved himself from falling by thrusting out the hand holding the pistol, felt it slide along the opposite seat in a slick of blood. The little drummer reached for him with fumbling, bloody hands. D'Arragon jerked up the pistol, the look in his blazing eyes stopping the drummer cold. Then, still down on his knee, he shot out his left hand and grabbed the girl's wrist.

'You're coming with me.'

'Oh, no, damn you — !'

The drunken cowboy said laconically, 'I don't think so, pal.'

A pistol had appeared in his hand. His unshaven face was still amused, his eyes lazily hooded, but the pistol was rock steady, the hammer back at full cock.

Thoughts flashed through D'Arragon's mind like birds fluttering in panic. Freedom was the click of a door away, a short leap down into the hot Arizona dust. Imlach was still out, his breathing stertorous; the fat drummer was paralysed by fear; the lean drummer was blood-soaked, and either stunned, cowed or prudent.

There was only one man in his way.

With a hard jerk that drew an angry, choked-off protest from the girl, D'Arragon pulled her off the seat, stepped across the centre bench and spun her so that she was a human shield. Her arm was twisted painfully up her back. Her pale, shocked face was turned towards the cowboy with the pistol, and the muzzle of the .45 D'Arragon had taken from the cattleman was held high to probe with deadly intent in the glossy dark hair behind her ear.

'Drop that pistol,' he said softly, 'or the girl's the first to die.'

And the coach ground to a halt.

In the sudden, eerie stillness, D'Arragon braced himself. He pulled the girl with him as he took a step to his rear and drove his booted foot in a powerful backward kick at the door. It burst open with a splintering crack, and swung wide to slam against the Concord's basswood side panels.

'You up there,' he yelled. 'Throw down the shotgun, any other weapons you're carrying. Then you, driver, climb down and cut loose two horses.'

For a few moments there was a deathly silence, broken only by the jingle of metal, the blowing of the horses, the creaking of the coach.

Then, unfazed, belligerent, the driver called, 'I guess that shot means Imlach's dead?'

'Nobody's dead, nobody'll come to any harm if you do as I say.'

'Oh, and what about that poor man?' The girl twisted her head, looked at him with naked contempt.

'Regrettable, inexcusable, but I had no choice.'

'You're a coward.'

'If that's another word for desperate, so be it.'

'Where are you taking me?'

'Far enough to put a lot of miles between me and — '

'You don't stand a chance, my father — '

'That's enough.'

The drunken cowboy laughed softly. There was a click as he lowered the hammer, a thud as the pistol hit the floor.

'He's holding all the cards, darling; I'd guess your pa's no closer than Yuma — and that ain't close enough.'

'All any of you need to know,' D'Arragon said, 'is that right now *nobody* can help you.' Then, louder, 'There's too much quiet out there, not enough movement. I'm giving you the count of ten, driver.'

'He's bluffing,' the girl called, then broke off with a strained gasp as D'Arragon applied pressure to her arm.

'The count's reached three,' D'Arragon shouted.

'Ma'am,' the driver said, 'I'd hate to risk — '

'Six . . . Seven — '

'All right, hold your horses, I'm comin' down.'

'First, the weapons.'

The coach rocked. Then there was the flash of slanting sunlight on metal, a heavy clunk, and D'Arragon glanced backwards to see the guard-messenger's shotgun lying in the dust. As he watched, Imlach's rolled-up gunbelt came fluttering and flapping to join it. The coach rocked again, creaking, and with a grunt the elderly driver jumped down and stood spread-legged as he glared at D'Arragon.

'The horses,' D'Arragon said. 'Cut two loose, fashion hackamores and bosals from the reins.'

'What d'you take me for, a — '

'Do it!'

Tom Gaines glared some more, spat, then tugged his grease-stained hat tight down on his head. He took a bone-handled knife from his pocket, opened the blade, and walked towards the front of the coach. That carried him out of D'Arragon's sight. The guard was still up on the box, as quiet as an Indian's ghost, the only weapons thrown down a shotgun and the marshal's .45.

D'Arragon was acutely aware that, in the coach's doorway, his broad back was exposed, the girl but a fragile shield between him and the dangerous cowboy with the loaded pistol at his feet. The muscles in his back crawled. He pulled her towards him, felt the stiff resistance in her slim body; wrestled her tight up against his chest, let go of her wrist, crooked his arm around her throat then took the pistol away from her head as he turned in the doorway. As he did so, out of the corner of his eye he caught the sudden, blurred shift of light as the cowboy's hand flashed towards the fallen pistol; felt the coach sway violently as the guard-messenger at last made his move.

3

Flint D'Arragon went backwards out of the Concord. He carried the young woman with him, broke her fall with his hard frame as he hit the sun-baked earth with his shoulders, heard the breath whistle from her body then pushed her away and rolled. When he came up on his feet in a boiling cloud of dust his left hand was again holding her wrist with a grip of iron. Without glancing at her he snapped a blind, warning shot into the coach's dark interior; against the blazing orb of the western sun saw the guard standing on the box with pistol up and swinging. Then he dragged the woman to her feet and into the shadows to flatten his back against the Concord's hot panels.

'That's enough!' he roared. 'You want the woman to live, back off. Guard, throw down that pistol. Now.

And you in there — hell, cowboy, didn't you already tell this young woman I'm holding all the cards?'

For several long moments it was as if seven people listened silently and unimpressed to the fading echoes of D'Arragon's words. Then, in quick succession, two pistols spun through the hot air and hit the dusty ground.

'That's me out of it,' said the cowboy.

The guard-messenger said, 'On your own, you stand a slim chance, feller. You take that girl, you'll have every lawman, every soldier, every Injun tracker in the territory on your trail.'

D'Arragon laughed bleakly. Then he said, 'You got those horses ready, driver?'

'I'm workin' on it, fast's I can.'

'I'll need a lead rope, too.'

'When he's done all that,' the young woman said boldly, 'you have to get me up on one of them.'

'One way or another,' D'Arragon said, 'upright or belly down, it's your choice,' and he moved with her into the dazzling sunlight and watched the driver fashioning hackamores and bosals from the slick leather reins.

The little drummer, snuffling through the blood, said, 'The marshal's coming to his senses.'

'Pick up that gunbelt,' D'Arragon told the girl.

She looked at him with cold blue eyes, seemed on the point of refusing, then thought better of it and bent to scoop up the looped belt and holster with its pouched .45.

'Fasten it around my waist.'

'With one hand?'

He grinned, shifted his grip from wrist to upper arm, held her firmly while she did his bidding. Then he looked in at the little drummer.

'Take off your boots, and your pants.'

'What the — '

D'Arragon silenced him with a glance, watched him step down from the coach and unbuckle his belt, then switched his attention to the girl.

'He's your size and build. When he's

done that, put them on.'

Then Mick Imlach was in the doorway.

'She can wear pants or a frock, you can take one of those guns or all of them,' Imlach said, 'and a lot of good it'll do you. You're a doomed man, D'Arragon. Let the girl go, die on your own like a man.'

He was standing loose limbed and unsteady, a rawboned man in middle age with blood in his grey hair and staining his face and shirt. He took a breath, stepped down shakily, began to walk towards D'Arragon.

'No further.'

The marshal stopped, swayed. 'You'll knock me down again?'

'If necessary.'

'Or threaten to kill the girl?' This with curled lip.

D'Arragon shook his head. 'It's over, Marshal. Leave it at that, ride on with the coach to Yuma.'

'Yes, I'll do that.' Imlach nodded, took an unsteady sideways step, leaned back against the coach. 'But you're wrong. It's not over, this is not the end, it's the beginning.'

'Beginning? That has a fine ring to it.'

'Savour it. Your time's short.'

D'Arragon looked into the level grey eyes, saw in them the hardness of tempered steel, then turned away as the driver approached leading two lathered horses trailing makeshift hackamores. They halted, wheeling and backing as he held them, blowing softly in the hanging dust.

The little drummer was standing self-consciously in his socks and underwear, his cotton pants in his hand. The young woman went to him, kicked off her shoes, took the bloodstained pants from him and pulled them on under the gingham frock's skirt, then donned his supple leather boots.

To the driver she said, 'Give me your knife.'

Gaines opened the blade, handed the knife to her. She took hold of the frock, poked the blade through the material at the waist, then with one smooth, strong motion ripped it all the way round and dropped the severed skirt on the ground.

D'Arragon watched her with sudden admiration. He saw her recognize the look and dismiss it, saw the contemptuous curl of her lip as she tugged at the ragged hem of the makeshift blouse, took hold of the hackamore and swung lithely up on the horse's bare back.

As a thought struck him, D'Arragon looked up at the guard, said, 'If you've got blankets in the box, throw down a couple, feller,' and waited impatiently for them to come flapping down, stinking of dried horse sweat. He rolled them, draped them across his mount's withers. Then, aware of eyes watching him, a wave of resentment and hatred that was almost palpable, Flint D'Arragon turned his back on the Concord, swung up behind the blankets and, with the lead rope held firm in his hand, led the way at a fast canter towards the forbidding landscape to the east.

4

'Four horses, a pistol and a shotgun,' Sheriff Dave Regan said, and glared. 'You could have taken two of the horses, the stage would have made it here anyway, and you'd have been after D'Arragon with a spare mount and armed to the teeth.'

'I thought about it,' Mick Imlach said, 'but there were complications.'

'Fran Parker?' Regan shook his head. 'All the more reason for sticking to that bastard like a burr to a blanket.'

'Too risky.'

'Hah! Tell that to John Parker when he gets here.'

'Flint D'Arragon murdered the owner of a bank in Redrock. With a man like that holding his daughter hostage, I reckon Parker will want some say in how we handle this.'

'*Some* say. But in the end it's down

to you and me, Mick.'

'Right. And my decision was to let him run, give him some rope.'

'Jesus!'

The two men, lawmen from different towns many miles apart but because of their jobs much more than nodding acquaintances, were in the small office above the jail on Yuma's lamplit main street. Regan was seated with his elbows on his desk, smoking a thin cigar, hat tilted back on his thick black hair, florid face glistening. Imlach was teetering in a straight-backed chair. His shirt was stiff with dried blood. Rough stitches showed in the white of his scalp where a patch of hair had been shaved by the doctor, and his lean face was drawn.

And in a chair alongside the iron safe, so far with nothing to contribute that would be of any value, lounged the coach's driver, Tom Gaines.

'All right, so which way will he run?' said Regan, as cigar smoke curled in the glow of the oil lamp.

'I picked him up on the San Pedro, took him back to Redrock. Criminal Sessions Court was held in the hotel lobby under Judge Blake. The bank's cashier was a reliable witness, the jury took thirty minutes to come up with a guilty verdict. D'Arragon was sentenced, I left Deputy Marshal Jim Fine to run the ship and boarded the stage with my prisoner. It was one hell of a trip — '

'Twenty-four hours, baking hot.'

'Right. And we almost made it. Then two hours from Yuma, and that stupid bastard let D'Arragon see the pistol he'd sneaked aboard . . . ' Imlach broke off, shaking his head.

'So now he's . . . what? Pushing his horse hard towards the Mex border?'

'Maybe.'

'Something wrong with that?'

Imlach pursed his lips. 'Bank robbery in Redrock, he was camped on the San Pedro — looks like he was heading east.'

'But now he's a convicted, hunted

36

killer, and Redrock's a couple of hundred miles away, the border no more than twenty. I've telegraphed ahead, they'll be keeping watch there in case he does back-track — '

'And those four men I mentioned came by the stage, two white, two Apache, they listened to the story and said they'd keep their eyes and ears open.'

'What was that feller's name agin?'

Tom Gaines, gnarled and grizzled, was leaning forward in his chair with his narrowed blue eyes glinting in the lamplight.

'The big man?' Imlach said. 'Scarface, lank blond hair?'

Gaines nodded.

'That was Pike Rickman.'

'You know him?'

This was Dave Regan, asking the question that was to be expected from any lawman worth his salt.

'No. He introduced himself, but I've never seen him before today, nor heard of him,' Imlach said, 'but by God he's not a man I'll forget too easy.'

Tom Gaines was looking at Dave Regan, his face wooden as he shifted a wad of tobacco from one whiskery cheek to another. Then he shrugged, and again sat back and lapsed into silence.

'Right, in addition to this Rickman feller there're scouts out there, Indians amongst 'em.' Regan grinned mirthlessly. 'We know he won't head this way — hell, he'll stay well clear of Yuma. All right, high-tailing north's another possibility, but if I was asked to put money on it . . . '

Imlach watched the sheriff light up a fresh cigar. He caught the flash of bright light as the flaring match flame was reflected in the shiny tin badge, winced slightly as pain stabbed at the back of his eyes, and said quietly, 'He had me wondering, D'Arragon, all the way from the San Pedro to Redrock, then for most of that infernal trip on the stage: wondering how a man could rob a bank, then eight hours later get caught cold, yet empty handed.'

'He buried it,' Regan said bluntly. 'Every last dollar. And that's something we'll talk about when we catch him — as we most assuredly will.'

'But if he stole the money, then buried it,' Imlach said, 'why run south for the border?'

'Hmph.'

Imlach's thin lips twitched in the hint of a smile. 'Doesn't make sense, does it?'

Dave Regan squinted thoughtfully at a point six inches above Imlach's head, sucked his teeth, then looked quickly towards the door as feet pounded up the wooden stairs and a big man entered the room.

Big in every way, Mick Imlach thought, as John Parker planted his hat on the desk, smoothed his sleek white hair, dragged up a chair and sat down. Big in stature, big in personality, by all accounts a hugely influential cattleman — and Imlach, a lawman from another town, had been unable to prevent a convicted murderer from taking his only daughter hostage.

One word to people in high places in Redrock, Imlach thought ruefully, and a hitherto unblemished career lies in tatters. And what about Dave Regan, a peace officer in this man's town . . . ?

'Sent for you as soon as the stage got in, John,' Regan was saying. 'Mick got his wounds stitched, told me the sad story while Doc was wielding his needle and thread, and I guess Will's already given you the gist?'

Will Smith, the gaunt deputy who had followed John Parker into the room, nodded, and went to the window overlooking the street. As he did so, Parker began to assert his authority by raising what was, to him, the heart of the problem.

'What will happen to my daughter?'

Sheriff Regan took a deep breath. 'John, we — '

'Marshal . . . ?'

'Mick Imlach, from Redrock,' Imlach

said. 'And I confess I just don't know, Mr Parker.'

'Well, I know my daughter. She's being held hostage, but she's tough and resourceful and will take full advantage of opportunities that occur.' He looked searchingly at Imlach. 'But what about the man who abducted her?'

Imlach spread his hands. 'Convicted of bank robbery and murder, on his way to the pen still fiercely protesting his innocence. That's one side of it. But his reputation as a gunslinger's based mostly on rumour, not fact, and instinct was telling me I was escorting a non-violent man. Then this . . . ' He touched the white patch of scalp, grimaced.

'You'll live,' Parker said bluntly, 'my daughter may not.'

'Then we'll move now, John,' Sheriff Regan said. 'Ride hard through the night, cut the feller off before he takes her across the border — '

'That's if he's headed that way,' Imlach cut in.

Parker looked from Regan to Imlach, then back to the sheriff. Regan shrugged, his eyes unreadable.

'Mick arrested him on the San Pedro west of Redrock, figures if D'Arragon was running in that direction then, that's the way he'll go now.'

'Because?'

'Because the money's not been recovered,' Imlach told Parker. 'It must be stashed somewhere close to where D'Arragon was picked up, and I don't think he's the kind of man to walk away from it.'

'Well, he outsmarted you once without too much trouble, was astute enough to take a pretty hostage he figured would make hotheads with blazing guns think twice, and be easy to keep hold of . . . ' He laughed softly at that, and Imlach felt anger stir within him as the big man sat nodding slowly, lips thrust out, brow furrowed in thought. 'All right, although you've made a hash of things so far I think I've no option but to trust your judgement on this — '

'Stringer's outside, Mr Parker, your fine sorrel horse all saddled up,' the deputy said from the window, an edge of sarcasm in his voice.

Parker stood up. 'Then we're ready to go.'

'Stringer?' Imlach looked at Regan.

'Runs the livery barn. I guess John figures his regular mount's not good enough for a manhunt, so he's got the old feller to bring along something special.'

'Nothing will be left to chance,' Parker said loftily, 'for however long this takes. We'll be riding hard and fast, possibly for several days and nights.'

'We all need fresh horses,' Imlach said. 'That's understood, and my question didn't imply criticism.'

'So let's get this straight, Regan,' Parker said, deliberately turning away. 'We ride now, four of us — and we ride *east*? We forget the border, because Marshal Imlach is convinced our man's sure to go back to the San Pedro to pick up that cash.' His dark eyes had turned to fix on Imlach. 'We ride through the night like the devil's on our tails, because we know where this man's going and we're going to run him down like a dog.'

Imlach met the big man's gaze, held it despite the dull ache in his head, then nodded once.

For an instant Regan hesitated, and Imlach felt sorry for the man. If Parker rode with the lawmen, Yuma's sheriff was being asked to carry out what looked like an impossible task under the eagle eyes of a powerful man who could, with a few harsh words of censure, take away his badge. Then Regan, too, nodded.

'You've got it, John. Will can stay behind, look after the store so to speak. And Mick Imlach's right: Flint D'Arragon's going for the money, not the border — and we're going after him.'

And with a decisive gesture he ground out the thin cigar, came around the desk and reached to the wall peg for his gunbelt.

★   ★   ★

But that wasn't the end of it. Before they rode out, on the darkened stairs leading down to the street, the coach driver, Tom Gaines, took Marshal Dave Regan by the arm and whispered into his ear — only the second time that evening the grizzled old-timer had opened his mouth to speak.

The first time he'd asked a question. This time he passed on information. And if Marshal Mick Imlach of Redrock had been privy to that information, he would have been a very worried man.

5

He pushed the horses at breakneck pace for almost a mile, tormented by memories of other reckless rides away from other violent encounters, his back crawling with rivulets of cold sweat in anticipation of the bite of hot lead, his only desire to put as much space between himself and his pursuers . . .

Pursuers?

D'Arragon laughed harshly, twisted to look behind him as he pulled back on the hackamore. The horses, already lathered from hours of hauling the heavy Concord, were stumbling from exhaustion. A young woman whose name he did not know had been crying out to him for several minutes, telling him to slow down — yet he'd heard nothing. And behind him, hidden by dust and the tortuous twists in the trail that snaked back through the rocky

46

terrain towards the setting sun, he'd left nothing more dangerous than a guard-messenger with a shotgun that was a useless weapon except at close range, and a bloody-headed, unarmed marshal, stoic still, but reeling with weakness caused by the wicked blow that had addled his senses.

'When they get that Concord moving, it'll be towards Yuma,' the girl said, drawing level with him as he let his mount sway to a head-hung, wrung-out halt. 'You're safe enough for a while yet, friend, so let's set a spell and work this out.'

She didn't wait for his reply. Almost open mouthed at her audacity, D'Arragon watched her swing down from the horse, leave the hackamore trailing and walk through the settling dust to the cool shade on the eastern side of a stand of huge barrel cacti. The horse followed, wearily, found its own resting place, let its head droop. And with a wry smile and shake of the head, D'Arragon stepped down

47

and joined the girl.

'No food, no water, and sundown's almost on us. Whose bright idea *was* this?'

'I guess I take the blame,' D'Arragon said, 'but in mitigation I'd ask you to use your imagination: I was a shackled prisoner looking ahead to maybe forty years in a sweltering cell in the Arizona penitentiary. What would you have done?'

'Never mind me. Are you guilty? Did you rob that bank, murder Amos Grant, the owner?'

'When it happened, I was nowhere near Redrock.'

'A reliable witness, a senior cashier called Vinny Price who was the only official in there with Grant, placed you there in the bank.'

'You know an awful lot.'

'I read the newspapers.'

'So you know the robber was masked.'

'Bandanna pulled up over his nose?' She shook her head slowly. 'If I were to come across you next week, next month, masked like that, I'd still recognize you from your eyes, the way you walk, the sound of your voice.'

'Of course. That's because you've seen me, spoken to me. But I told you, I wasn't in Redrock at the time, so how did this reliable witness, this Vinny Price, recognize a man who wasn't there?'

She stood up, frowning, reached into her boot, unclasped the driver's bone-handled knife and sliced into one of the fleshy cacti. She squeezed the pulp, let the sap dribble into her hand, moistened her lips and looked hard at D'Arragon.

'Are you suggesting this fine, upstanding cashier was involved in the robbery?'

He looked into her eyes, searching for sarcasm, saw none and said, 'When I get to Redrock, that's the question I'll be asking.'

She laughed at the idea, thought for a moment and said, 'Following on from that, if the cashier's guilty, the man who walked into the bank was his accomplice. They were in cahoots?'

'Not man. Men. There were two of them.'

She tossed the knife to D'Arragon, watched him catch it and slice into the cactus, squeeze the pulp and tilt his head back to drink.

'I guess the newspaper I read missed that.'

D'Arragon shrugged. 'A quick-thinking cowboy crossing the street downed the second where he stood at the hitch rail, holding the horses, his eyes fixed on the bank. But a dead outlaw's not news unless he's notorious. No, all folk were interested in was the man with the smoking shotgun who came backing out of the bank holding a gunnysack — '

'Backing out?' She raised an eyebrow. 'Sounds like you *were* there.'

D'Arragon's smile was bitter. 'Let's say I have been — but not this time, and never in a Redrock bank.'

'All right. So who would hate you so much they'd go to all that trouble, take those risks, to send you to the pen? One man died, you say, so they paid a heavy price. Why not just put a bullet in your back some other time, some other place, and walk away?'

'Pure chance,' D'Arragon said, though even as he spoke he knew it sounded implausible. 'Robbing the bank was why they rode into town. But then somehow they discovered I was in the territory and not too far away, got the idea of pointing the finger, shifting the blame, at the same time settling an old score.'

'Do you know what that was?'

'If I knew what, I'd likely know who, but my only lead's that cashier.'

She nodded, looked around uneasily at the gathering gloom. 'And if you're telling the truth, a murdering bank robber's on the loose, maybe hating you tenfold for the loss of his partner.' She wrapped her arms around the thin material covering her shoulders, and shivered. 'But there's a big if in there. What I've seen in the past hour is a convicted killer viciously pistol-whip a marshal, steal two horses and take a woman hostage — and unless something happens to tip me the other way, your story of a crooked cashier involved with two bank robbers who, for some damn reason, want you framed for murder is just so much hogwash.'

'Then ride with me,' D'Arragon said, 'of your own free will. So far all witnesses are speaking against me, and I need that to change.'

In the sudden, strained silence D'Arragon was aware of a harsh, rocky terrain stained blood-red by the dying rays of the sinking sun; the shadows of the cacti like dark, clawed fingers reaching out across the ground; the silhouetted crags and ridges, jagged, black and daunting, behind any one of which a cold-hearted gunman might even now be lining his rifle's sights on D'Arragon's chest.

There was an urgent need to find

sanctuary for the night, even if the temporary haven was no more than a rocky overhang, a stand of parched trees — perhaps a shallow depression in open ground offering scant cover but impossible for marauders to approach without being detected.

'You say of my own free will,' the young woman said, breaking into his thoughts, 'but do I have much choice?'

'Mount up, let's find somewhere to make camp,' he said gruffly.

It took fifteen minutes of slow riding through the gathering gloom before they rounded a high bluff and came across a grove of stunted cottonwoods on the parched grass banks of a dry wash that snaked down a steep slope. The dried-up water course emerged from a notch high up the hill where rimrock was split like the V of a huge gunsight. On either side of that notch the ridges were starkly outlined against the luminous night skies. Below the cottonwoods, the wash petered out and the land fell away sharply in a broad expanse of loose scree.

'This is safe enough,' D'Arragon said. 'If the posse comes in above us, I'll see them. If they approach from below they'll make enough noise to waken the dead.'

'Always supposing,' she said, 'that there's anyone out there,' and he thought briefly about a woman's intuition, caught the sudden tension in her voice then, for the moment, pushed possible reasons for it to the back of his mind.

This time when they dismounted, D'Arragon fashioned rough hobbles for the horses — using the driver's sharp blade to cut lengths off the hackamores — and led them to a hollow where the grass showed some green. In amongst the trees the rustling detritus of countless passing years became indistinguishable from corn-husk mattresses when the horse blankets taken from the Concorde were spread; folded back over their bodies, the other half of those

54

same blankets afforded shelter from a chill, cutting night breeze.

Under the sparse canopy of the cottonwoods they lay looking at skies awash with stars. Their bodies were separated by several feet of dried leaves and mouldering branches yet, D'Arragon knew, in the direction their thoughts were taking they were as close as kindred spirits. He could smell the sourness of his own drying sweat, the lingering taste of rank cactus juice was in his mouth, but the bitterest taste of all came from the knowledge that his impetuous, violent actions — no matter what the motive was — had been wrong, were still wrong. Inevitably, those thoughts were weighted down with regret; just as inevitably, for the sake of his sanity, he hunted for crumbs of justification and followed his thoughts into a box canyon from which there seemed no escape . . .

'What you were thinking,' he said softly, remembering her tension, 'is that, before too long, if there is anyone out there, it's just as likely to be your pa.'

'John Parker,' she said out of the darkness.

'And you are?'

'Fran.'

'Your pa's rich, Fran?'

'And powerful.'

'Yes, but there's a limit to what power can achieve. We rode away from the stage no more than an hour ago, it'll take another hour for it to reach Yuma. Say, once it gets there, it takes your pa a couple of hours to raise a posse. That makes it three hours from now before they're even ready to ride.'

'No matter how long it takes, he'll make it.'

D'Arragon smiled bitterly up at the stars.

'That's been my philosophy for as long as I can remember. I was orphaned at fifteen, rode out the same day with a six-gun strapped to my hip and right then I told myself, whatever it took, whatever I had to do, I'd make it.'

'I guess we now know what it took,' Fran said, 'and from what I read in those newspaper accounts, the only thing you made was a reputation.'

'Based on camp-fire tales told by men eager to bask in reflected glory, the lies of others desperate to hide their own guilt.' He realized his shrug of resignation would go unnoticed in the dark, and said, 'But I've lived that double life for too long to worry, now it's just a question of — '

His words broke off abruptly as, close by, a stone rattled.

He said softly, 'Was that you?'

'No,' she said, her voice tight with fear — and even as she spoke a hand stinking of rancid grease shot out of the darkness and clamped over Flint D'Arragon's mouth, and the sharp point of a knife pricked the skin of his exposed throat, drawing a bead of blood.

6

They built a smokeless fire on the edge of the cottonwoods, the bright flames dancing across the grubby white head-bands and swarthy faces of the two Mimbreño Apaches as they worked, but barely reaching the two white men who stood talking in low tones well outside the circle of flickering yellow light.

D'Arragon and the girl were sitting cross-legged with the fire's heat in their faces, forced there, forced down on to the hard flat stones and warned by jabbing gestures to be still and quiet when the Apaches dragged them bodily from their blankets and out of the trees into the chill breeze where a cold moon, still below the rimrock, was already illuminating the terrain with its wan light. There was blood drying on their throats for, from the moment they had pounced out of the darkness, the two silent Indians had got instant, unquestioning co-operation by painfully puncturing soft skin with their knives and making sure their captives felt the hot wet bite of the sharp steel.

'What do you want from us?' D'Arragon said.

'What do *we* want?'

The tall, lean man had shoulder-length hair the colour of sun-dried straw under a flat-crowned black hat, a thin horizontal scar resembling Apache war paint across the bridge of his nose and both high cheekbones. He stepped into the firelight, his deepset eyes like slivers of colourless glass. They'd weep tears as cold as ice, D'Arragon thought, while he strangles a new-born calf with his big hands, and he felt a chill of fear.

'It's others that want,' this man went on, his voice a breathless rasp. 'Word's out: there's a killer on the loose. Ain't much more been said, no specifics, but I'd guess there's a reward . . . ' He shrugged, leaving the consequences of such an offer to D'Arragon's imagination as he hitched his low-slung six-gun and moved closer to flick the end of his cigarette into the flames.

And D'Arragon's imagination was running wild. First thoughts when the Indians pounced and dragged him and the girl before the two white men were that they'd fallen foul of marauding desperados, the girl would be raped, and when that was done they'd be searched for valuables then dumped in the wash with their throats slit. Instead, it seemed the two white men had figured out who he was, knew of his conviction, and were sniffing at the possibility of a reward like vultures circling beady-eyed above the rotting carcass of a steer.

Well, better the rough night ride to Yuma with even the slimmest chance of escape than a bloody death under the slashing knives of the Indians — yet something was wrong, something didn't sit right, and for the life of him D'Arragon couldn't put his finger on it.

He watched as the second man signalled to the Apaches, and all three men drifted silently away into the long, boulder-cast shadows and up the steep dry wash. Several silent minutes later, an uneasy span measured by the spaced crackling of the settling blaze and the restless pacing of the tow-headed man, harness metal jingled and several horses were led down slope and taken to where D'Arragon and the girl had left the hobbled stage horses.

'Timing's not right,' D'Arragon said at last, breaking the long silence as he looked at Fran Parker then confronted the tall man. 'We left stage not much more than an hour ago. No way word could've reached Redrock or Yuma, no way you could have got here in that time from either of those towns.'

'You're not thinking straight.' The tall man tossed the makings to his partner as, breathing hard, face moist, he walked into the firelight. 'Supposin' we were already hereabouts, goin' about our lawful business? Supposin' we happened on that stage and its scared passengers, spoke to Marshal Mick Imlach — lookin' bloody and a mite pale around the gills — listened to what he had to say and told him, leave it to us, your troubles're over?'

'Is that the way it was?'

'How else could it be?' the tall man said, 'if I've accurately described Marshal Imlach's current state of health.'

'And does it matter a cuss,' said the second man, 'one way or the other?'

'Maybe he's fussy 'bout who takes him in, sees him locked up,' the tall man said.

The man working on the makings was as dark as the tall man was fair, with a floppy black hat drooping over lank hair and his heavy jowls covered by several days' growth of black beard, a man stocky and muscular in a way that put severe strain on the few buttons holding together the threadbare shirt worn under a black vest shiny with age.

He finished rolling his cigarette, lit it, the match flame flaring bright in eyes like wet black stones.

'We ain't flashed no badges,' the dark man said, and blew a jet of smoke. 'Maybe if we had tin stars, he'd be reassured.'

'Or maybe,' the tow head said, 'he's worried about the lawfulness of that business I said we was on.'

'That's something that bothers me a lot,' Fran Parker said. 'If you really are taking this man on to Yuma, why am I getting the same harsh treatment?'

'Oh, we're taking him all right,' tow head said. 'And I can assure you, ma'am, this time he won't get away.'

'You haven't answered my question.' She stood up, stretched, looked at them defiantly and said, 'And do you have names?'

'Pike Rickman,' tow head said. 'The feller with the laughin' eyes is Blackie Donovan, and those two' — he grinned — 'well, those two're Apaches.'

'Maybe I'm missing something here,'

D'Arragon said, frowning as he routinely searched his memory, 'but those names don't set any bells ringing.'

Rickman's colourless eyes were blank. Enigmatically, he said, 'What's in a name? Back in the 70s, a man calling himself Charlie Bolton could slip away unnoticed 'less someone let slip the innocent-looking gent was the notorious Black Bart.'

'But that was then, and this is now,' Fran Parker said dismissively, 'and before we ride for Yuma, I'd like something to eat.'

'Would you now,' Donovan said, and spat a shred of tobacco.

'Do you realize who my father is?'

'Ma'am,' he said, 'I don't know or care if you've got or ever had a father.'

'His name is John Parker,' she said, her face pale with anger — and Rickman and Donovan exchanged swift glances.

'You can introduce us when the time comes,' Rickman said, almost purring, 'and me and your pa will get together to discuss that reward.'

'The reward for capturing Flint D'Arragon?' She shook her head. 'That's not my father's concern.'

'No, but you've set me thinking,' Rickman said slyly, 'that a powerful man like John Parker is certain to cough up a whole lot more for the safe return of his daughter.'

'Ah!' She flashed a contemptuous look as sharp as daggers at Flint D'Arragon. 'Rather like you,' she said, 'these ruffians seize on any opportunity that will improve their lot, without any thought to the harm they might cause.'

'Which little mouthful,' Rickman said, 'just about sums up what's happenin' here, and puts an end to this pow-wow.'

'So we now know exactly where we stand?'

He grinned at D'Arragon. 'Sure you do. After a slight hiccough you're once again pointin' in the right direction, headin' for a cell in Yuma. An' pretty little Fran Parker's, she's suddenly become what you might inelegantly call cash on the hoof.'

'All right, that's it,' Blackie Donovan said. 'We'll rest thirty minutes, enough time for hot java, but no grub. That done we'll mount up, see how fast we can get this sorted out so everybody — exceptin' maybe Mr D'Arragon there — comes out of it tolerably happy.'

★ ★ ★

By the time they were ready to move out, D'Arragon estimated that it was pushing three hours since he and Fran Parker had ridden away from the Concord. That would put the coach pulled by its weakened team already an hour into Yuma, and although he had suggested to Fran it would take two hours to raise a posse, he knew that was taking little account of Mick Imlach's efficiency and determination. The gritty lawman's long experience would warn him time was of the essence. If he'd spoken eloquently, played on emotions but tempered his words with common sense, a posse would already be hammering out of Yuma. And with the two groups of riders racing towards an inevitable encounter, that left D'Arragon an hour at most to make his second break for freedom.

They clattered away from the dry wash with the rising full moon a yellow, baleful eye wedged in the gunsight that was the notch in the high cliffs, the riders' shadows cast long to their left flanks as they cantered towards the west. The two Apaches led the way, followed by Pike Rickman, then D'Arragon and the girl again riding bareback, with Blackie Donovan's formidable presence bringing up the rear.

But that suited D'Arragon. Mick Imlach's gunbelt with pouched six-gun had been taken from him in the cottonwoods when he was overpowered by the Apache, and was now looped over Donovan's left shoulder. Maybe the man figured wearing it like that befit a *bandito*, served as a deterrent — or maybe he just wasn't thinking. The fact was, if D'Arragon slowed, Donovan would be forced to drop back with him. If Fran Parker played her part and began to lag, they would become detached from Pike Rickman, and in those favourable if risky circumstances . . .

D'Arragon gave it a mile, then gradually picked up the pace and drew alongside the girl's horse. Rickman sensed his approach, glanced back, saw no danger and faced front. Donovan was less accommodating.

'Drop back, D'Arragon.'

'Just asking how she is.'

'She's fine. Now fall back into line.'

Fran's face was pale in the moonlight as she turned to look at him. Out of the corner of his mouth D'Arragon said softly, with as much intensity as he could put into the words, 'Begin to fall back from Rickman. Nothing sudden. Nice and easy.'

'D'Arragon!'

'All right, all right.'

He tugged lightly on the hackamore and brought his horse back to fall in behind the girl, then eased back some more. Gradually, Fran Parker did the same. Done in that way the two of them remained locked together, and they had covered almost a mile before Donovan realized they'd fallen a full 100 yards behind Rickman and the Indians.

'Keep up,' he growled, moving his horse up to crowd D'Arragon.

'We're riding stage horses, bareback. I'm feelin' it, and I don't think the girl can take much more.'

In weak moonlight that was broken up into irregular patches by the rough terrain there was no way Donovan could check D'Arragon's words without coming in close. He did so, using his horse's weight to shoulder push past and approach Fran Parker, at the same leaning forward in the saddle to look closely at the girl.

And it was at that moment that Rickman's warning cry rang out, his loud halloo coming to them as eerie echoes off the slabbed rock, assailing them from every direction.

'Riders, coming in hard and fast from the west!'

7

The warning was caught and carried away on the thin breeze, its echoes fading like an elusive, half-remembered dream. An answering shout came floating through the night: like a pack of wolves, the approaching riders had pricked their ears, caught the sound and the scent and were in full cry.

And already the small window of opportunity was slamming shut for D'Arragon. Far ahead, the two Apaches had melted into the shadows. Pike Rickman had swung his horse about and, at full stretch, was pushing it back towards the group.

Now — or the chance has gone!

With a mighty intake of breath, D'Arragon kicked hard with his heels. His horse started, leaped forward. Donovan was caught, wedged fast between the two stage horses as

D'Arragon clung to the hackamore, heaved his horse across hard into the big man and pulled to a halt. Then, swiftly, he leaned across, twisted his body and slammed his elbow in a terrible blow across the nape of Donovan's neck. The man grunted, and started to go down. D'Arragon caught his left arm, lifted it, wrenched the looped gunbelt from the dazed man's shoulder. Then he swung again with his elbow, another vicious, pole-axe of a blow, and knocked the big man out of the saddle.

'Stay here,' he said to the girl. 'That'll be your pa coming, you're safe now.'

Her face was pale in the moonlight. 'Don't run away,' she said. 'Truly I don't know what to believe, but running is no answer and I'm willing to talk to my pa, get him to listen to your story — '

But Rickman was hammering towards them, light glinting on a six-gun held high, and D'Arragon reached across to touch her shoulder as he swung easily from the bareback of the stage horse into Blackie Donovan's saddle. His right knee brushed a booted Winchester as the horse danced sideways; his boots found the stirrups as he held himself erect, buckling Mick Imlach's gunbelt. Then he picked up the reins and kicked the excited horse into a gallop and was away, swooping recklessly downhill as he raced towards a maze of gullies and ridges where wan moonlight fought a hopeless cause against deep shadow and a desperate man could choose from a hundred different routes and lose himself in each and every one.

8

'Ain't no one I know — but whoever he is, he's coming round.'

Dave Regan was down on one knee alongside a big man who lay flat on his back, rolled his head and blinked sightlessly at the stars. Mick Imlach was soothing the downed man's jittery horse while John Parker, still in the saddle, looked off into the night with tormented gaze. Sweat glistened on his face. His head was cocked. A long way off, like the lazy rumble of a far distant storm, there was the fading beat of hoofs.

Parker gave a perplexed shake of the head and reined his horse close to Regan. 'Leave him. We should be riding, not talking and wasting time on a ruffian who was up to no good,' he said. He was erect in the saddle. There was purpose and strength in his words, but Mick Imlach knew he was talking for effect, unsure what to do but intent on giving the impression that he was a man in full control of a difficult situation.

'A few minutes'll make no difference,' Regan said. 'It looks like this bunch was coming straight at us, heading towards Yuma. We'd already decided D'Arragon wouldn't do that, but we also know there are men out looking for him. This could be one of 'em. I'd like to know what's going on.'

'I don't agree,' John Parker said. His horse was swinging its stern, tail switching as if it sensed Parker's impatience. 'Whoever this feller's companions are, they hightailed when they heard us coming. I say we push on.'

'Wait.' Mick Imlach could understand Regan's lack of observation, he had gone straight to the downed man and was giving him his full attention — but he would have expected John Parker to see at once what was staring

75

him in the face. 'This feller was riding bareback,' he said. 'So what does that tell you?'

'My God!' The businessman swung out of the saddle, stepped around Regan and the semiconscious man, reached out to the restless horse and grasped the bosal to hold it as it backed away. 'Are you saying this is one of the horses taken from the stage?' He ran a hand absently down the nervous horse's neck, thought for a moment, then shook his head in disbelief. 'No, Marshal, D'Arragon and my daughter were riding those horses, that can't be right.'

'I watched the driver use a pocket knife to cut his reins, make that hackamore. There's no mistake.'

'But this is not Flint D'Arragon?'

'Hell, no.'

'So what are you saying? What does it mean?' He looked from Imlach to Regan, his frown demanding answers, the look in his eyes telling both lawmen he was out of his depth.

Dave Regan sat back on his heels. 'Common sense is telling me D'Arragon set your daughter free, John, and pushing for home riding bareback over this rough terrain she got thrown — but then we're left explaining this feller here, and suddenly I've got a bad taste makes me want to spit.'

He leaned forward, grasped the man's shirt front and pulled him to a sitting position. As he came up, head lolling, Regan slapped him across the face, twice, hard, forward and back. The man swore softly, groaned. He reached up, tried to rub the back of his neck. His eyes blinked open.

Regan placed a bony fist under the man's chin, held the head steady, then thrust his face close.

'Sheriff Dave Regan,' he said, 'out of Yuma,' and grinned coldly into the wet black eyes that were still glazed. 'Talk fast, feller, start with your name, then tell me why I shouldn't hang you for riding a horse stolen from Hatch & Hodges.'

'Donovan,' the man said hoarsely.

'And . . . ?'

'The last thing I remember, the man riding that horse was crowding me, hitting me over the head with something felt like a fence post.'

'Flint D'Arragon!' John Parker said bleakly.

'That's right. We found him and the girl, were bringing them in,' Donovan said, and turned to look blearily at Imlach. 'I saw you earlier, remember, before sundown? You were at the stage, as groggy then as I am now.'

Imlach nodded, mentally cursing his own lack of observation: he didn't know Donovan, but should have recognized him from the stage, and he caught himself wondering if it would be construed by Regan as a deliberate slip if things went wrong. 'I remember. You, that tall, scar-faced feller with hair to his shoulders, two Apaches. You came by, promised to keep your eyes and ears open.'

'That's right, me and Pike Rickman.

And we did.' Donovan nodded vigorously, then winced and held his neck. 'The Apaches picked up their trail, we ran them down then held back and waited till they rolled their blankets in some cottonwoods on the edge of a draw. Then the Injuns moved in and caught them cold.'

'Wouldn't it have made sense to hold off longer, wait for daylight and help?' Imlach said, biding his time, thinking it through, knowing that this man was using portions of the truth to mask something much deeper.

'The way things turned out,' Donovan said, 'hindsight's telling me we should have left them where they slept and rode straight on. But we'd given our word,' he went on with an unctuous smile, 'and we all knew the right thing to do, the honourable thing, was to take that killer on to Yuma.'

Regan had gone to his horse, and now came back holding a heavy canteen. Donovan took a long drink then rested, hands dangling between spread knees as if exhausted. To Imlach, it was a pose. The man's strength was returning fast, but he was doing his best to feign weakness. Instinctively, from long experience with his kind, Imlach knew he was sure to cause trouble, but until the man slipped up, made some kind of move . . .

Then John Parker spoke up in a way that made Imlach warm to the big businessman.

'Sorry, feller, but your story's as full of holes as a Californian miner's sieve,' he said bluntly.

'Yeah, sure,' Donovan said scathingly. 'I was out walkin', found this horse wanderin' loose, rode into a tree and knocked myself out.'

'All right,' Parker said, 'then what about the girl? What about my daughter?'

Donovan shot the big man a quick, calculating look, then strove in vain to look blank. 'What about her? She was with D'Arragon.' He shrugged, tossed the canteen to Regan.

'This is the picture I've got,' Mick Imlach said carefully. 'You and this Rickman apprehended the fugitive and his hostage, set out for Yuma, D'Arragon took his chance, knocked you senseless and got away — on your horse?'

'That's it, exactly,' Donovan said, and almost sneered at Parker. He struggled to his feet, stood swaying for a moment, then straightened and thrust out his massive chest. 'And being an honourable man just like me, my partner — figurin' I'm not too bad hurt — he turns around and goes after him.'

'Then why take the girl?'

'Huh?'

Regan was also up on his feet, his hand drifting close to his six-gun, the gleam in his eye telling Imlach that his question had got to Donovan and knocked the ground from under his feet.

'If D'Arragon had split seconds to overpower you, take your horse and make his getaway, he would have left the girl behind. So why has your partner taken Fran Parker along for the ride?' Regan said, hammering home the point Imlach had made. 'She'll slow his pursuit of D'Arragon, there was an injured man here to be looked after — you, my friend — and in any case she was so close to Yuma she could near as dammit walk there.'

For an instant the man called Donovan seemed to be searching for an answer that would take away the heat. His eyes were lowered, but shifty, flicking from one lawman to the other then off into the shadowy moonlight.

Weighing up his chances, Mick Imlach thought — then tensed and dropped into a crouch as, with a muttered curse, Donovan turned as if to walk away in disgust and stabbed a hand for his pistol.

Regan was too close, too fast. A short stride brought him level with Donovan. His six-gun came out, up and down in one smooth movement, and the dull thud as the barrel hit Donovan's shoulder caused Imlach to wince with cloudy memories of an earlier gun whipping. Then Donovan was bent over, cursing softly. His limp arm swung helplessly, his hand close to his holster but incapable of grasping the pistol's butt. The nervous horse was shying and backing away to the length of the hackamore as Parker grabbed for it and hung on.

'Seems like I was right all along,' the big rancher said when the dust had settled, and his jaw muscles were bunched as he faced Regan. 'We've been wasting valuable time; in doing so allowed D'Arragon to get even further ahead — '

'But now your daughter's not with Flint D'Arragon,' Imlach cut in.

'As good as!' Parker swung away, fuming, swung back again to stab a finger at the two lawmen. 'This man's actions were those of a violent man riding on the wrong side of the law. His partner will be cut from the same cloth — and you believe that man and two savages now have hold of my daughter.' He paused to catch his breath, his eyes inward and withdrawn as he gathered his thoughts, then went on in a more reasonable tone but with a noticeable quiver in his voice, 'A young woman, all alone, held captive first by one man, now by three. And we're wasting time in pointless talk.' He glanced up at the cold orb of the moon, shivered, said quietly, 'If you're right, Marshal Imlach, D'Arragon's making for the San Pedro and that stolen cash; and we all heard this man's partner's heading in that same direction. I think that tells us what we must do.'

Mick Imlach took a breath. Parker was stating the obvious, but he was right about time being wasted so maybe it needed saying. He looked at Dave Regan, and nodded.

'Right, let's go get them.'

9

Within five miles, Flint D'Arragon was lifting his eyes to the night skies in silent prayer as Blackie Donovan's horse finally snorted wetly, wearily, and refused to take another step.

D'Arragon had not pushed him hard. Instead he had used the undulating, scarred terrain and its vast areas of deep shadow to make his way steadily east, threading his way through arroyos and dry washes, riding with his shoulder brushing the rocky walls — doing everything he could to put difficulties and obstacles in the way of Pike Rickman and the two Apaches, because there was no doubt in his mind that the rawboned man would lead the chase. So he picked his way carefully, treading a fine line between the softer ground where dust drifting in the moonlight would betray him, and the flat slabs of rock where dust was no problem but the hard ring of the horse's hoofs would carry far through the night.

But the big, heavy man who had been astride this horse before him had ridden him into the ground, and it was that merciless ill-treatment that had taken its toll. The horse was worn out, tendons taut, muscles sore and quivering, and it was with a feeling of raw bitterness tinged with a good measure of sympathy that D'Arragon slid from the saddle, ran his hand absently along his lathered mount's streaming neck and took stock of the situation.

After downing Blackie Donovan he had cut away from the confusion and ridden steadily, without haste, putting concealment before reckless speed. He had glanced over his shoulder several times but there had been no sign of pursuit, and he guessed that, if it was John Parker at the head of a posse hammering down the trail from Yuma, Rickman and the Indians would need time to talk to them, Donovan a spell to recover and Parker a few moments to decide what to do with Fran. But that would not delay them for long and, with D'Arragon now forced to rest his horse for several hours, the race to Redrock seemed lost, his own freedom in jeopardy.

Yet even if, somehow, he eluded the men now hunting him, his future was bleak. If the bank cashier whose testimony had convicted him had done a deal with the bank robbers, he was unlikely to stick around for too long with money weighing down his pockets and a rope waiting for him if he began gabbing. Without him, D'Arragon faced at best a life on the run, always one step ahead of the law — and knowing that the time left for him was now slipping away like sand through an hour glass, he looked quickly around him.

The moon was high, lighting up a wide, shallow depression from which rocky slopes rose easily on three sides;

on the fourth side, the hollow was bounded by one of several trails D'Arragon had used — no more than a deep run-off cut by winter rains tumbling down from higher ground. If he was forced to remain there, his shelter would be gnarled trees, chiselled boulders as big as small cabins, the inevitable stark contrast of light and shade.

But a desperate man could make much out of nothing.

D'Arragon's restlessly ranging eyes had already picked out a steeper slope leading to a small, flat-topped spur where tumbling boulders had lodged precariously to form a huge, protective rampart, and stunted trees clung to the naked rock. At the back of the spur the cliff face rising to the rimrock was vertical and, beneath it, shadows were at their deepest.

D'Arragon cocked his head, and nodded slowly, and with satisfaction. There were still no warning sounds carried on the thin breeze, and even as he listened, even as his mind instinctively leaped ahead along the tortuous route he would ride and the evasive action he must take if the posse reinforced by Rickman and the Indians appeared out of the night and he was forced to make a run for it — even then he was coldly planning details of the stand he knew must make, there, in the moonlit hollow.

He grinned savagely. Moonlit. That was the key. He had to make a stand, because with an exhausted horse he was left with no alternative; in such circumstances light of any kind was preferable to pitch darkness; and because there were, as yet, no riders tearing after him down the winter run off, he had time to prepare.

Murmuring softly to the exhausted beast, D'Arragon walked it down to the very centre of the hollow where the moonlight was at its brightest. There he hobbled it, off-saddled and dumped the rig on the ground, and swiftly gathered enough rocks to make a small circle.

Inside the circle he built a fire. As kindling he used coarse dry grass; on top of that he carefully spread more grass dampened thoroughly with water from the canteen he found in Donovan's saddle-bags; on that, he lay twigs and thicker branches broken from the stunted trees.

The snaps of breaking branches were like gunshots, the sharp sounds would carry far; and he caught himself smiling as he applied flame to the kindling, for if the snaps were interpreted as shots those shots would confuse, and confusion could only help his plan. So D'Arragon watched the flames catch, saw the kindling fiercely heat the damp grass, listened to the hissing as clouds of smoke began billowing and, suddenly acutely aware that, no matter what was to come, at that moment he was a free man, laughed out loud with a joy that was rich and uninhibited.

Then, sobering, he dragged the saddle closer to the fire, went to the dozing, hip-shot horse and removed the blanket, from that blanket and more coarse grass moulded a bulky shape that could pass for a man sleeping with his head on the saddle. Then he slid Blackie Donovan's Winchester from its boot and backed off several yards to survey his handiwork.

What he saw was a man sleeping by the fire, rolled in his blankets. He slept close to the blaze for protection from marauding animals, for a different reason altogether had laid his bed in the open under clear moonlit skies: illogically, he believed that made it difficult for the men chasing him to creep up on him undetected. So there he lay in untroubled sleep. Alongside him, his horse dozed. Blackie Donovan's horse. In full view.

With a grunt of satisfaction, D'Arragon turned and jogged across the hollow and up the slope and on to the flat spur, slipping behind the rocky ramparts and into shadows where the cold descended like an icy shroud to chill his face and the vista, as he turned, was like that enjoyed by a Roman emperor perched high above an amphitheatre where men fought savagely. And men would fight, here, if D'Arragon had judged the situation aright — and, even as that grim inevitability took hold and became lodged in his mind, he caught the distant clack of hoofs on stone, listened hard and detected just two horses and was at once puzzled.

He sipped tepid water from Donovan's canteen, frowning, looking across the hollow to the run-off. Two men approaching seemed to suggest Rickman, a recovered Donovan on the stage horse D'Arragon had abandoned — and no posse. Which in turn suggested what? Either the riders coming from Yuma had been others with no interest in D'Arragon and they had ridden on through, or it had been the posse and they were playing cagey by sending one man on ahead.

But Pike Rickman and Donovan would be with the posse, and they would use the tracking skills and fighting abilities of two Apaches. So, D'Arragon thought uneasily, setting the posse aside for a moment, another way it could be played was for Rickman and Donovan to ride boldly down the draw to attract his attention while the two Apaches sneaked in silently from the flanks. If the Indians could overpower him with their stealth and their knives, the posse's task would be made easy.

And even as those thoughts crossed his mind, a faint pale flicker on the far edge of the clearing caught his eye.

Goddamn!

He put down the canteen, cursed silently as it toppled over with a faint metal clink; saw the pale blur melt away as if it had been pure illusion to leave nothing but the mysteries of the empty hollow, the shape that could have been a man sleeping by the fire.

How much had he given away? Had the clink of metal on rock carried clearly? Was the Apache close enough, his hearing sharp enough to locate the true source of the sound? Or had his

93

black eyes looked across the clearing to the fire's smoky flickering and imagined movement in the rolled blankets, seen in the flames the glint of metal as the drowsy man fumbled for his canteen?

If that, D'Arragon thought, then his ruse was working better than expected. But it was no more than that, a subterfuge, a delaying tactic. Sooner or later the deception would be uncovered, the rolled blankets and grass tossed aside, and then the Apaches would turn away from the fire and begin to use their inherent, unrivalled skills in the hunt to track him down. And if the eyes of a mere white man had within seconds been drawn to the slope leading to the natural fortress on the flat-topped bluff . . .

At the edge of the hollow, a figure seemed to rise from the earth. Under a dark headband, slitted eyes were fiery sparks in the moonlight. A cavalry carbine was held low and, as D'Arragon watched, the Apache padded silently and sinuously forward on moccasined feet. Making straight for the fire.

D'Arragon's breath hissed softly through his teeth and his hand clenched on the Winchester's stock. There, beyond the fire, thirty yards back, the second Apache. And he was coming in low, hands and feet wide to support his body as he hugged the ground. The cold blade of his knife glinted in the moonlight as he matched his pace to that of his companion, inching forward, always watching, patiently waiting for the man by the fire to scent danger and come rolling out of his blankets with eyes wide and sixgun cocked and swinging.

And now the approaching horses were very close.

D'Arragon shot a glance towards the edge of the clearing, looked up the slope of the run-off, squinted so hard his eyes watered as he strained to see beyond the moonlight and into the far shadows. He saw movement, caught the sheen of light on a lathered horse's coat, the flash of yellow hair under a flat-crowned black hat; saw a second horse following, on it not Blackie Donovan but the much smaller figure of another dark-haired Apache in colourful cotton shirt —

No!

Dammit, the two Apaches were here hunting him, the one on his feet and strutting now close enough to be a ghostly figure wreathed in smoke from the flickering fire, the second like a deadly insect flattened to crawl across the moonlit hollow with a glittering blade between his teeth. So, it was Pike Rickman coming down the draw, yes, but not Donovan, and not an Apache. Instead it was someone much smaller, someone with dark and lustrous hair long enough to sweep slight shoulders, someone wearing what looked like a shirt of colourful cotton but which was in reality the remains of a gingham frock D'Arragon could even now hear tearing under the pressure of two strong hands —

Fran Parker!

And suddenly the situation had changed dramatically.

The condition of Donovan's horse had forced him to make a stand in the moonlit hollow, but tacit in his decision had been the promise to himself to make no move against any man working with the law unless he was cornered; already he had violently assaulted a lawman, stolen two Hatch & Hodges horses and kidnapped a young girl, and enough was enough. He had expected a posse. Instead, he was looking at a man who had ridden out of the night to hunt down an escaped convict and transport him to the penitentiary at Yuma, then spoken openly of holding Fran Parker to ransom when he learned that her father was rich and powerful.

Something was wrong. Only a gullible fool would continue to believe Pike Rickman was working for anything other than his own ends. And that being the case, D'Arragon was no longer bound by his promise.

It was time to take the initiative.

Tight-tipped, his eyes on the Apache now close enough to see details of the inert shape through the flames, D'Arragon jacked a shell into the Winchester's breech and took aim.

10

Shocking in the stillness of night, the shot seemed to freeze all movement, drain the colour from the landscape, catch and hold a man's breath. For an aching, endless moment it seemed that time stood still. Then, like a hanged man suddenly cut free, the Apache crumpled to the ground. One outflung arm dropped across the fire, producing a shower of bright sparks that were caught and carried on the breeze.

Not a back shot. D'Arragon allowed himself that small consolation, while mentally grieving from the knowledge that he had killed a man in cold blood, without any warning. But the torment brought by that admission of guilt was short lived. As the shot cracked out across the clearing the second Apache had dropped flat. The muzzle flash would have been dazzling, revealing

D'Arragon's position. And it would also have been seen by Pike Rickman.

D'Arragon was now aware that in the instant of stillness following the snap of the shot, there had been a flurry of movement in the dry wash. The two approaching horses had suddenly been lost to view, moving swiftly away and dropping into a small arroyo.

Now, from that cover, a rifle cracked. A bullet smacked into the cliff face above D'Arragon's head. Slivers of stone hummed wickedly. At the same time, down in the hollow on the other side of the fire where the dead Apache's arm smouldered, the second Apache sprang to his feet and set off in a crouching run away to D'Arragon's right. He was making for a dip in the ground that would take him out of D'Arragon's sight, offer another hidden approach to the flat-topped spur.

Icily, without feeling, D'Arragon dropped him in his tracks with a single shot. The Apache went down, rolled, and lay still.

Which left Pike Rickman.

But Rickman, it appeared, was having second thoughts.

A second shot rang out from the arroyo, the bullet whispering close to D'Arragon before ricocheting from the rocks and whining wickedly into the distance. But the horses were already moving, rattling away down the draw, always out of sight. The hoofbeats receded, dwindled; silence once more settled like a thick blanket.

Carefully, Flint D'Arragon eased himself upright. As he did so — as he emerged from the shelter of the boulders to look down on the moonlit hollow where an exhausted hobbled horse stood with ears pricked and the whites showing in its frightened eyes and the shape of a man was still undisturbed by the camp-fire where two Indians lay dead — he thought about the rattle of gunfire that would have carried on the night air, the posse that was sure to be within earshot and, with a soft exclamation of chagrin tinged with uncertainty, he started down the slope and into the unknown.

★ ★ ★

'Shooting,' Dave Regan cried from up front. 'Comin' from the south.'

Mick Imlach pulled off the track and reined in. His head was cocked. As the others milled, brought their horses around and back to him, he looked at Regan.

'If that's who you think it is,' he said, 'then he's not heading for Redrock.'

'Hah!' John Parker exclaimed. 'So much for trusting your judgement.'

'Don't jump too fast,' Regan said. 'If a man wanted to lay a false trail, he'd do something like this. Twist and turn. Head one way, give himself space then swing on to another tack.'

'So what's he run into?' Imlach said, and twisted in the saddle to look at Donovan.

'Rickman and the Indians have caught up,' the big man said sullenly.

'If that's so,' John Parker said, 'my daughter's slap bang in the middle of a gunfight.'

'Shooting's finished,' Regan said, eyes bleak as he looked off into the moonlit distance. 'If this Rickman is a citizen doing his duty, we'll meet him on the way back. If not . . .'

'One way to find out,' Parker said, and with a final glare in Imlach's direction, he swung his mount and raked it with his fine Mexican spurs.

He flung it at a gallop off the trail, heading for the maze of arroyos and dry washes that fell away to the south and which had been noticed but avoided by the two lawmen. Now, with a glance at each other, they swung into line with Blackie Donovan wedged between them and spurred after the businessman.

Parker's big sorrel had covered the ride from Yuma without sweat, and took off down the slope like a winged avenger. Twisting and turning like a big cat on the rocky terrain, it carried the big man away from the other three riders, leaving them to eat his dust. And so it went on, mile after mile, Imlach taking up the rear and using the comparative isolation to marshal his thoughts, still concluding that he was right about D'Arragon, but admitting that he was in the dark about Rickman's intentions.

Three miles, four miles, at breakneck pace. Then into the fifth — and they were up with John Parker, who had come to a halt. Again they milled, this time swinging around the big businessman who was reined in on the edge of a shallow basin where a campfire smouldered, a hobbled horse watched nervously, and two ominous white shapes lay in the dust.

'My horse,' Blackie Donovan growled.

'And if I'm not mistaken,' Regan said, 'your redskin companions have gone to the happy hunting ground.'

'D'Arragon was riding that horse,' Imlach said. 'Where is he?'

'Gone with Rickman,' Donovan said.

'Why leave your horse?'

'Wrung out,' Donovan said, and shrugged. 'Those two Apache horses'd be around. D'Arragon's riding one, they've got a spare.'

'But we didn't meet them coming back,' Dave Regan said, 'so where the hell have they gone?' and the question went unanswered as John Parker touched the sorrel with his spurs and rode down into the shallow depression.

'Stranger and stranger,' Mick Imlach said. 'You throw any more light on this, Donovan?'

He shook his head and slid down off the bony bare back of the Hatch & Hodges horse. It trotted away, going after Parker and skirting the camp-fire to approach Donovan's horse. Imlach and Regan followed, came up with Parker as, still mounted, he moved away from glancing at the second Indian's body and glowered down at the rolled blankets lying close to the fire.

'Easy to see what happened,' Regan said. 'They closed on D'Arragon when that horse faded, he had time to rig a trap.'

He looked around, saw the slope leading up to a flat-topped bluff, nodded thoughtfully. 'If that's where he holed up, they smoked him out, but not before he plugged those two Apaches.'

'Rickman would have sent them in,' Donovan said, and laughed. 'Lookin' after his own skin.'

'So where is he?' Parker said tightly. 'Where's Flint D'Arragon, where's Rickman gone with my daughter? According to you, Imlach, D'Arragon was heading for the San Pedro; according to this feller, Rickman was doing his damnedest to bring him to Yuma. Well, seems like he caught him, but all we can see for sure is a camp-fire with a dummy, two dead Indians, and the stink of gunsmoke.'

'We know we didn't pass 'em on the way here,' Dave Regan said, 'which suggests they've headed for the border away to the south.'

'Or the San Pedro, where D'Arragon stashed the bank's money,' Mick Imlach said. He looked at Donovan. 'Is that what happened? You and Rickman had just caught D'Arragon and the girl, were arguing over the takings from the bank job when we came along and D'Arragon took his chance to break away. Now Rickman's got hold of him again. They're heading for the San Pedro, aren't they? They'll either split the cash, or Rickman will take the lot.'

Donovan shrugged. 'Either way, count me out. I'll not ride bareback again. You go haring after them, just leave me here.'

'Do that,' Parker said to Imlach. 'He'd only slow us down. But you've figured it right. Figured it the only way. I couldn't see any of this feller's kind putting themselves out to bring a bank robber to justice. Looked at this way, everything makes sense — including Fran being taken along: the Indians are out of it, D'Arragon and Rickman have formed an unholy alliance and my daughter's their insurance.'

'Or more cash on the hoof,' Imlach said softly, and saw the shock in the businessman's eyes. 'Come on,' he said, 'we're wasting time.'

★   ★   ★

He watched them go, Blackie Donovan, hunkering down by the fire as they rode off, stirring the dying embers with a stick and thinking about his aching head and sore rump and his thirst and the water bottle in his saddle-bags. And the strong coffee. He grinned in the moonlight, rolled sideways to come up on his knees, pushed the rolled blankets aside and tugged at the saddle. But when he unbuckled first one bag, then the other, he discovered that his canteen had gone — and so had his rifle.

His smile faded. Suddenly he was conscious of his awkward position, and felt the hairs on his neck stiffen. Then he heard the unmistakable rattle of a rifle's mechanism, and froze.

'Nice and easy now,' Flint D'Arragon said. 'Turn around slowly, and put your hands where I can see them.'

11

The fire was spitting and crackling again, flames leaping and dancing in the fickle breeze as Blackie Donovan piled on gnarled, dry branches and the peeling bark caught and flared like thin parchment and sparks flew wild and free.

'I was listening back there,' D'Arragon said, hunkered down upwind of the blazing camp-fire with the Winchester close to hand. 'I heard enough to know Imlach and the rest of them have got it wrong. There were no arguments between you and Rickman over stolen bank takings; it seemed to me Rickman's only concern was seeing me locked up for life.'

'Who the hell cares?' Donovan said, back to prodding the fire. 'I'm out of it, glad to see the back of the man.'

'How come you got involved in the first place?'

'Hired gun. Rickman had a job to do, would take a while and so he figured he'd need help. I happened to be drinking at the same Redrock bar and looking for some easy money.'

'What job?'

'Like you said: making sure you got to Yuma, seeing you clapped in a cell and the key thrown down the nearest mineshaft.'

'So it was no chance encounter, you'd been shadowing the stage?'

'Every hot, dusty mile.'

'Saw me make the break?'

'Sure.'

'Then why not move in then, back up the lawman? Why let me ride free with the girl and risk losing me for good?'

'For Rickman, it was always personal. When you cut loose he no longer trusted the law to hold you.' Donovan looked up, black eyes glittering in the firelight. 'The girl was a hole card, once he got his hands on her. You? Hell, all he wanted was to deliver you to Yuma, watch you locked up, listen to the door clang shut and spit in your face.'

D'Arragon nodded slowly. There was no reason for Donovan to be lying, and his story simply reinforced D'Arragon's foreboding: Rickman had not ridden away, accepting defeat, but had watched with fury as the Apaches were gunned down then prudently and swiftly withdrawn from a situation where a marksman armed with a rifle was holed up in a natural fortress. But that was surely temporary. He would listen, watch and wait — might even now be perched somewhere up the rocky slopes looking down on a hollow where two men talked by a blazing camp-fire over which the moon shone wanly. When the time was right — he'd pounce.

But why?

He looked at Donovan. 'For Rickman, it was personal — that's what you said. But what did you mean? Is Rickman a ghost out of my past, some deepseated grudge burning a hole in his brain?'

The big man shook his head. 'No.

But the feller killed in the Redrock bank robbery was Rickman's brother.'

'Jesus!' D'Arragon climbed to his feet, picked up the rifle, walked off to stare into the distance, then came back to stand close to the fire where the wafting heat seared his face as his mind whirled dizzily at the shocking news. Rickman's brother had been killed in the bank robbery for which he, Flint D'Arragon, had received a life sentence. Bad enough — but if the brother had been outside the bank, holding the horses, then the other man involved had to be Pike Rickman.

'Pike Rickman,' D'Arragon said, fighting to think through the throbbing at the back of his eyes, 'was the second man at the Redrock bank. The man inside. The man with the shotgun. That makes me the innocent man sentenced for Pike Rickman's crimes of robbery and murder, the fall guy, the man taking the rap — and now we've got to the real reason he was desperate to ride herd on me all the way to Yuma.'

'I didn't say that.' Donovan shook his head. 'Didn't say he was involved; don't know either way, never risked thinking about it. Rickman wanted you put away because he blamed you for his brother getting plugged during that robbery. Put away, not dead, so you'd spend the next forty years or more paying the price. That's all I know, and I'm in a hurry to forget that and everything to do with that crazy man.'

D'Arragon snorted. 'How the hell could he blame me?'

'Because,' Donovan said, 'you were in Redrock and you shot your mouth off.'

And suddenly it became clear. As D'Arragon backed away from the heat of the fire, sat down crosslegged on the fringe of the flickering light and caught the tobacco sack the big man tossed to him, he remembered the night in a Redrock saloon, his idle remarks to the saloonist about the town's bank being ripe for the picking, the guarded look in the man's eyes as he listened without apparent interest.

The man was a saloonist, a small-town lawman's listening post, and he would have talked. D'Arragon's words would have been repeated, and remembered by listeners because he had talked about the possible robbery of a bank where their money lay — and it had been Rickman's terrible misfortune to have planned just such a robbery for a day when the townsfolk and the law in Redrock had been put on the alert: by D'Arragon, and his idle talk while passing time.

The match flared. D'Arragon blew smoke, tossed the Bull Durham sack to Donovan. As he savoured the bite of the cigarette, wry amusement stirred, for he was now in the curious postion of being a hunted man who found himself in the wilderness somewhere behind the hunters. The trackers were about to be tracked, and could lead him all the way back to Redrock.

But not Rickman. Rickman was out there, watching, of that D'Arragon was convinced. And for every hour the man was frustrated, the danger increased. He was a man who'd committed a bank robbery, the cash from that robbery must be waiting for him somewhere in Redrock, and eventually he would reach the conclusion that chasing after D'Arragon was pure waste of time when a bullet in the back would serve the same purpose, and remove all risk: with D'Arragon dead, any doubts about his guilt would be forever buried.

'I'm taking your saddle, and rifle,' D'Arragon said, and flicked his unfinished cigarette into the fire. 'Come to that, your black hat and shiny vest will change my appearance enough to get me by in a dark room. The stage horse will carry me to hell and back. Yours will do the same for you, when it's rested.'

He felt the big man's eyes on him as he prepared to move out, but it was not until he slid the Winchester into its boot and swung into the saddle that the terrible risks he was facing hit home. He was setting off to trail a posse of which one member would happily shoot him on sight. To follow them without being seen, while thwarting Pike Rickman's efforts to capture him, he would need the guile of a fox and eyes in the back of his head.

With a final nod to the silent, watchful Donovan, knowing he was setting out on a perilous ride with all the odds stacked against him, he touched the stage horse with his heels and moved out of the hollow.

★   ★   ★

Dawn was a blaze of sunlight over the eastern mountains, searing light that spanned the endless horizon and turned the world into a dazzling panorama drenched in rich ochre and pure gold but forced a man's head down so that he rode blind with his hat tilted and his trust placed squarely on his sure-footed pony.

By the time that brilliant dawn broke, Flint D'Arragon was through Gila

Bend and pushing across the eastern fringe of the Gila Desert towards Casa Grande but, as his night-chilled body soaked up the warmth that arrived with the sun, he knew that with the dawn there came danger. For, when first light was but a ghostly luminescence and the sun's fiery rim was yet to push above the distant peaks, he had looked ahead and picked out in the distance the thin, hanging plume of dust that was like an arrow pointing to a group of riders pushing towards Redrock. Predictably, the posse had ridden hard through the night believing that D'Arragon was ahead of them. Now, with the daylight, they would continue to scan the trail ahead for a lone rider but would also begin watching their back-trail, and it was in that indefatigable watch by hardened lawmen that danger lay.

By a narrow creek trickling down from the high rocks, D'Arragon paused to swill his face with water like melted ice that brought a fierce ache to his throat as he drank deeply, then climbed to a vantage point and gazed into the west where the sun's heat was peeling back the flat banks of white mist from the desert and the darker vegetation away to the north. Nothing. No movement. No dust marking a chasing rider's position the way it marked the posse. And it suddenly occurred to D'Arragon as he wasted precious moments rolling and lighting a cigarette that in all probability Pike Rickman had bedded down for the night, for in that man's mind there would be no urgency. He would be unaware that Blackie Donovan had revealed at least a part of his guilt, would be unlikely to suspect that D'Arragon and Fran Parker had discussed the cashier and his almost certain involvement in the robbery. If he thought at all about D'Arragon's intentions he would almost certainly presume his quarry was heading east simply because he had been riding in that direction when arrested and was resuming his interrupted journey, and with that knowledge he would be confident that he must eventually ride him down.

It was even possible that during the hours of darkness he had done some hard thinking and given up the chase. Why work himself into a lather hunting a convicted man when a posse was doing the job for him? Why place himself within a hundred miles of the law when he could split the money with the cashier — if that worthy was involved — then vanish into the western badlands knowing another man was serving time for the crime he had committed?

Such thoughts were a considerable comfort to Flint D'Arragon. He sucked happily on his cigarette, gazed with satisfaction at the vast expanse of stillness that lay behind him, then turned again and from his high vantage point looked with some amusement at the plume of dust marking the ever-changing position of the posse that had stayed ahead of him during the night and was chasing a phantom.

Then, with a decisive flick, he sent the cigarette sparking into the damp grass. With a final glance west he turned and started down towards his horse — and froze.

In the thin mist that still curled on the stony banks of the creek, two men were watching him. Guns glittered in their fists. Tin stars winked in the sunlight. And as hopes that had been sky high plummeted like a stone tossed into a bottomless well, as euphoria faded as inexorably as the morning mist, D'Arragon looked down to his left where another more powerful man waited in patient silence, then lifted his eyes to the plume of dust that he now knew marked the position not of the posse, but of Pike Rickman and Fran Parker who had ridden past him in the night.

12

Suddenly, Pike Rickman's hole card had taken on the value of a gold nugget for a Flint D'Arragon bankrupted of all hope. Had it not been for Fran Parker, Mick Imlach of Redrock would have handed D'Arragon into the custody of Marshal Dave Regan of Yuma, and they would have commenced the long hot ride to the state penitentiary.

Instead, after his subdued descent from the vantage point and the surrender of his weapons, a fire had been lit hastily, breakfast was sizzling in a blackened pan alongside an equally well-used coffee pot, and the prospect now was a fast ride in the opposite direction — east — exactly the direction D'Arragon wanted to take.

Sure, he was proceeding that way under armed escort. And yes, although the posse's aim now was the rescue of

Fran Parker, inevitably, when that was completed, the delayed matter of the convicted murderer and his trip to the pen would be dealt with. But D'Arragon well knew that time was his most valuable asset, there was likely to be considerable confusion when the three hunters came up with Pike Rickman, and if D'Arragon couldn't make something out of that when the time came, well, maybe he deserved locking up.

So he hunkered down and chewed the tough fried beef, drank the strong coffee and watched the fretting John Parker and, while openly sympathizing with the distressed father of the kidnapped girl, his thinking was telling him that Parker was the key to his escape. The man was a tight spring looking for release, and as such unpredictable. When the big man finally caught up with the scar-faced owlhoot who was holding his daughter, there would almost certainly be an explosion of violence as Parker snapped and lost control. In that split second, and the ensuing moments of uproar and chaos, the captive Flint D'Arragon would be forgotten.

Mick Imlach was watching him closely, seemingly intuitively reading his thoughts, and now he said, 'I guess you knew what you were doing when you gunwhipped me, took the girl.'

'No,' D'Arragon said. 'I didn't. And I've come to believe it was wrong. Right to make the break, wrong to take the girl, but when a man's looking a life sentence in the eye — '

'For a crime he didn't commit?'

That was Dave Regan and, at his words, John Parker turned away in disgust and walked to his horse.

'That's right,' D'Arragon said. 'Convicted for something I didn't do; of robbing a bank when I was fifty miles away.'

'Innocent, but you couldn't prove it.'

'Wasn't given the chance.'

'My guess is you're full of big talk, if you'd had the chance you'd have been stumped to find the right words.'

'Then, yes. But not now.'

Imlach sent the coffee dregs hissing into the fire, then looked hard at D'Arragon.

'So in twelve hours of freedom and most of that darkness, you've come up with something new?'

'Some of that time was spent with a couple of owlhoots masquerading as law-abiding citizens. One of them came up with a name. I now know the man shot dead outside the bank,' D'Arragon said, 'was Pike Rickman's brother. Rickman wants me locked up because he's grieving for his brother, figured my loose talk led to that killing. And right now Rickman's riding hard some five miles ahead of you — because he believes I'm ahead of him.'

John Parker swung around, his eyes wild. 'What else do you know?'

'I'm pretty certain the bank cash-ier — '

'Forget that, what about this Rick-man,' Parker said savagely. 'What do you know about him; what kind of a man is he?'

'Fran let slip you had money. That cheered him up, set him talking about a ransom.'

Dave Regan swore softly.

'What was that about the cashier?' Mick Imlach said, his eyes strangely hooded as he watched D'Arragon.

Parker exploded. 'For Christ's sake — '

'Wait, John,' Regan said. 'We're going after Fran, no more time wasted, I promise you, but while we're making ready we can hear this.' He was up on his feet, gathering the hot cooking utensils while Imlach kicked dry earth over the glowing coals.

'You know damn well,' D'Arragon said. 'The cashier was the witness present at the robbery who came forward at that mockery of a trial to point the finger.'

Imlach nodded, seeming to relax a little. 'Not surprising. A day earlier you wore a mask, he looked into your eyes over the barrel of your shotgun,' he said. 'Something like that gets seared into a timid man's memory.'

'If you're right, all he saw was the bank robber's eyes, yet when you brought me into town from the San Pedro he was hopping about in front of the bank and identified me from fifty yards away with the sun in his eyes.' D'Arragon watched Imlach, let him digest that, dig deep in his memory, saw the man's eyes narrow slightly. 'Who pointed you towards the San Pedro, Imlach?'

The lawman laughed shortly. 'Who'd you think? Jake Creedy, the man in the saloon looking after your thirst, the man who listened to your wild talk about bank robbery and Redrock being ripe for the picking.' Imlach finished saddling up, saw the others were ready, looked at D'Arragon. 'That it?'

D'Arragon shrugged, swung into the saddle. 'I can understand Jake. I let my tongue run loose, said too much. But when we get to Redrock I'll talk to that cashier — '

'Like hell you will,' Imlach said.

'Right!' John Parker's exclamation was scornful. 'We'll be finished with this Rickman feller within twenty miles, turning right around and taking you straight back to Yuma and locking you up for life with my girl safe and well.'

He was already swinging his horse and pulling out, throwing the bitter words over his shoulder. Dave Regan followed him, Imlach gestured to D'Arragon who pulled his horse in behind the Yuma sheriff's, and the four men kicked their horses into a fast canter and headed into the sun in a strung-out line with Imlach taking up the rear.

The cashier, Flint D'Arragon thought. I must make it, talk to the cashier. If I can't find him, then I hang on to Rickman's tail and the scar-faced man is certain to lead me to him.

And, as the riders settled into their rhythm and the dust billowed and he plucked at his bandanna and pulled it up over his mouth and nose, he found himself first smothering a smile at the image he must be creating for the two lawmen, then letting the smile expand into a full grin beneath the mask as he unashamedly rooted for Pike Rickman and urged the gaunt outlaw on to Redrock.

13

Pike Rickman became aware of the pursuit as the last of the night mist faded into memory and the heat of the sun brought the constant sheen of sweat to a man's skin and began sucking him dry. He picked up the yellow dust plume drifting stark against clear blue skies above the high ground a mile back, noted as he constantly twisted in the saddle the tiny dark shapes beneath that lazily trailing plume that added up to three or four men. And, as he watched, he began toying with the possibilities, calculating the whos and the whys and the wherefores and the implications, and all the while another part of his mind was casting around wildly for a way out like a beady-eyed rat cornered in a dusty barn.

'There ain't no way out,' he at last mused out loud, his words coming as an indistinct mumble in the monotonous drum of horses' hoofs. 'If it's the posse, sooner or later they'll run me down. When they do that they'll see the girl and then the whole effort — Redrock, the bank, D'Arragon, followin' the stage — won't be worth a damn.'

Listening, sensing the indecision in the man, Fran Parker said, 'Better to let me go. If I drop back that will delay them, give you your chance.'

She was suffering. The ridged backbone of the horse she had ridden bareback for many miles was cutting into her body, the hot sun already searing her skin through the thin top of the shortened frock. But her mind was alert and, as her heart began to beat a little faster at the knowledge that rescuers were slowly pulling them in and rescue was drawing ever closer, she began to work on the big man with the scar who had set out with companions and wound up alone.

'If you're going to set me free, do it

now,' she said. 'Why risk your life when you know you've already lost Flint D'Arragon?'

The two horses were still linked by a lead rope, but Rickman had shortened it so that she was now forced to ride alongside him to keep the rope slack. Conscious of him very close she kept her eyes fixed straight ahead but realized the shocking impact of her words as Rickman's head snapped around, his cold, colourless eyes fastened on her.

'What do you mean — lost him?'

'The posse has picked you up and they're running you down because of the dust trail you cannot hide. You looked back and spotted a similar trail on the high ground behind us — kicked up by their horses — and that gave them away.' She turned to him, her smile sweet. 'So tell me, where is Flint D'Arragon?'

'Up ahead,' he said hoarsely. 'He's up ahead, riding hard for the San Pedro, he *must* be — '

'What is he then, a ghost rider? There's no give-away dust trail that I can see, Rickman, so unless he's holed up somewhere, I think you're wrong. You know we came up on the posse in the night, rode past them when they pulled in to give their mounts a breather. I think we rode past D'Arragon, too, without knowing it — and if we did, and the posse picked him up — '

'No!'

'Isn't that what you want? Flint D'Arragon in jail?'

'Yes,' he said. 'All right, yes, that's exactly what I want — '

He broke off as Fran heaved on the hackamore and pulled the stage-horse's head back, jerking it to a stiff-legged halt. The rope linking her to the outlaw snapped tight. Rickman rocked forward in the saddle, grabbing for the horn as his horse took the dead weight of Fran's mount and stewed awkwardly.

'What the hell!'

'Listen to me.'

'I don't need — '

'Last night,' Fran went on insistently, 'you'd apprehended a convicted killer and were taking him in as your prisoner to hand over to the law. You were a hero. Today you've turned tail and you're running away from that same law, your prisoner this time a girl you kidnapped. What does that make you?'

'D'Arragon took you, not me!'

'But I'm not with D'Arragon, I'm with you, and from back there it'll look like you have no intention of turning me over to my father. You're riding the wrong way, one step ahead of the law and running for your life — and last night D'Arragon heard you laugh when you discovered my father is a rich man, heard you gloat when you thought of the money he was sure to cough up for my release.'

'Shut your mouth!'

'He'll have told Mick Imlach, told my father — '

'For the last time — '

'Do you want to die before you see Flint D'Arragon returned to prison?'

Rickman's eyes were wild. He glared at the girl, looked beyond her to the ominous plume of dust on the high ground, guessed that the men riding the horses kicking up that dust would be watching him through field-glasses, would know that for some reason he'd pulled up . . .

With a grunt he leaned back in the saddle and savagely tugged on the reins. His horse backed until the lead rope again snapped tight, this time rocking the girl so that she was almost unseated.

'Is that what you want?' Fran Parker said, gasping, clinging on, her eyes burning into Rickman's.

'What I want right now,' Pike Rickman said through clenched teeth, 'is to give those fellers back there something to make them sit up, something to drive home that this is no game we're playing.'

Thinking it through, knowing that,

even watched through powerful field-glasses, the dust and the heat-haze would make them indistinct figures almost lost against the dun-coloured earth, he deliberately drew his six-gun.

'What . . . what are you doing?'

'Weren't you listening? You all of a sudden gone deaf?'

'I — '

Rickman lifted the pistol and, as the girl watched him with wide, horrified eyes, he cocked it and fired. The shot sent flat echoes reverberating into the silence. As hot lead hummed past her ear, Fran Parker rocked on the back of the frightened horse. As she did so, Rickman again sent his horse hard backwards, yet again snapped the lead rope tight.

This time, the girl was unseated. As the echoes of the shot faded away into the distance, she toppled backwards and landed awkwardly on the hard, dusty ground.

★　★　★

It happened the way D'Arragon had envisaged, but a whole lot sooner than he'd expected and with raw emotion taking the place of violence. Or at least, taking the place of violence in which any of them could be directly involved. Maybe it was the unexpected that threw the two lawmen. Certainly the gods were on D'Arragon's side, for when the incident occurred the posse was descending a slope alongside thick woods that rolled away into the low hills to the north. Inexplicably, for no reason that D'Arragon could fathom, Imlach had chosen that moment to ride past him — with a secretive smile and a muttered 'Don't do anything stupid' — and pushed on fully fifty yards to where the Yuma sheriff had moved alongside John Parker.

Suddenly aware that this could be the moment he'd waited for, D'Arragon slowed his horse as his attention was grabbed by the drama unfolding up ahead.

John Parker yelled something hoarse

and unintelligible, turning in the saddle to the advancing Imlach and gesturing wildly. Following the direction of the waving arm, D'Arragon could see nothing with the naked eye — but an instant later he heard the faint crack that was the unmistakable report of a distant shot. Even as the flat whisper of sound reached him he saw Imlach stand in his stirrups, one hand holding field-glasses clamped to his eyes as John Parker madly put spurs to his horse and sent it pouring down the long slope at a reckless gallop.

Dave Regan was calling after Parker, while watching Imlach with half an eye and no doubt asking him what he could see, what the hell was going on — and why he'd left D'Arragon!

And without any hurry Flint D'Arragon took the opportunity handed to him on a plate by Mick Imlach, gently touched his horse with his heels, and took it into the cool, shaded silence of the woods.

PART TWO

14

What struck Flint D'Arragon forcefully as he slipped into Redrock was that he was a convicted killer riding back into the small town where people believed he'd robbed the bank and murdered its respectable owner — and that was exactly the way he looked. Since being taken from the hotel lobby where he'd been found guilty of those terrible crimes he had spent most of one day being tossed about like a loose sack in a dusty Concord, two nights and another full day riding rough across Arizona Territory with only a couple of hours' sleep to freshen him up, and the result was a wreck of a man who hadn't been near a straight razor in all that time and was looking at the world through red-rimmed eyes deep sunk in a gaunt, bewhiskered face.

Not only that, he thought wryly, but

he was riding a horse carrying the Hatch & Hodges' brand — and that added horse-thief to the crimes for which he could justifiably be strung up from the nearest tall tree.

He rode into the town when lamplight was losing the battle against the shadows left by the departing sun, and without any clear notion of what he was about to do he eased his horse up against the stripped timber walls of the tall livery barn and lost himself in the purple gloom.

Convincing himself that his freedom depended on nothing more than confronting a crooked cashier and putting everything to rights had been a fine way of keeping his spirits up when he was nearing the end of his tether, but when the outskirts of Redrock appeared as an insignificant smudge against the evening skies he realized he'd been clutching at straws. He didn't know the man's name or where he lived, asking questions around town was a sure way of getting himself arrested and, if that wasn't enough trouble, he had to face the possibility that the man was already long gone.

Successful bank robbers didn't get that way through hanging around. Raids were shocking in their brutality, gunny-sacks were hastily stuffed with cash at gunpoint, the getaway was organized and fast.

And yet . . .

The cashier wasn't a bank robber. His involvement — if D'Arragon was right — had been limited to the covert passing of information to the outlaws who walked into the bank. A day later he had been a witness at the short trial, and had testified against D'Arragon; he was a solid citizen holding a responsible position, and with the bank robber convicted and on his way to Yuma the man's stock was high — so why walk away?

The answer to that was easy: suddenly, inexplicably, a bank cashier had become very, very rich.

D'Arragon cursed softly. His thinking

was on a trail to nowhere, time was running out, and danger was all around him. Mick Imlach's deputy could appear on the street at any time, the townsfolk would lynch D'Arragon on sight, Pike Rickman was already in town with the girl and, from the soft whisper of sound that was causing the Hatch & Hodges' horse to prick up its ears, the three men D'Arragon had cunningly shadowed for most of the long hot day then slipped away from unseen and left in his wake in the run for town were now within half a mile of Redrock.

The lights of the jail office were fifty yards ahead of him to his right. As D'Arragon watched and tried to shrink deeper into the shadows, the office door opened and in the flood of light a man stepped out, scratched a match, applied it to a cigarette. Jim Fine, the deputy. D'Arragon felt his shoulders tighten. The horse, sensing his unease, moved restlessly.

Disturbingly aware of the insistent

drumming of approaching hoofs, D'Arragon leaned forward to soothe the horse with a gloved hand while looking about him with narrowed eyes and weighing up his chances. The street was empty, the windows of business establishments supporting rickety false fronts in darkness. The saloon across from the jail was brightly lit, but still quiet. Across from the livery barn where D'Arragon hugged the shadows, the entrance to the hotel where Judge Blake had passed sentence on him was dimly lit, and warmly inviting.

The hotel owner, D'Arragon recalled with a sudden, familiar surge of hope, had been away on that fateful day, the short hearing watched by a white-haired clerk who had wrung his bony hands in terror at the responsibility foisted on him on the day he was due to retire. D'Arragon needed a safe place to lie low. He would find none more suitable in the time left to him — and the approaching hoofbeats were now an insistent pounding like a nervous pulse in his ears.

The problem was the horse.

But not if he played his cards right.

It took him no more than two minutes to take the incriminating Hatch & Hodges' stage horse clattering on to the barn's dim runway, wave away the hostler who came limping from the lamplit office, then off-saddle and lead the horse into a vacant stall. When he emerged, the hostler was watching him, and for an instant as D'Arragon flipped him a coin he thought he'd slipped up; that he'd stabled his horse here on his last, fateful visit, forgotten the incident and, despite the change in appearance effected by wearing Donovan's black hat and vest, he was now about to be unmasked.

Then, even as he realized that memory was playing tricks on him and he'd given his horse no more permanent a resting place than the nearest hitch rail, it became irrelevant: as hoofs thundered and three riders dragged dust down the street and wheeled to a halt under the watchful gaze of the man smoking outside the jail office, the hostler turned away from D'Arragon, stepped outside and spat a stream of tobacco juice in the direction of the newcomers.

Once again, a watcher had been distracted, letting Flint D'Arragon off the hook. Quietly, unnoticed, his eyes always flicking towards the old man, he stepped inside the lamplit office, took a shotgun from the rack and a box of shells from the shelf. Then, outside again with the gun held tight against his side of his leg, he tugged Donovan's hat down low, slipped past the oblivious hostler and crossed the street to the hotel.

★   ★   ★

'An unsavoury character with lank blond hair and a scarred face, and a young woman riding a Hatch & Hodges' horse bareback,' Mick Imlach said. 'You seen 'em?'

Behind the desk in the jail office, sitting in Imlach's swivel chair, Deputy Jim Fine shook his head. 'If they came to Redrock they snuck in, kept to back alleys. If they're here at all . . . ' He shook his head to express deep misgivings, suggesting that locating the outlaw and his captive would be impossible, then looked with some sympathy at the big businessman who had turned away in disgust at the bad news.

'Maybe an hour ahead of us?' Imlach said, insistently nudging the deputy's memory.

'Or maybe still out there,' Dave Regan said, and Fine raised an eyebrow.

'He pulled a stunt,' Imlach said, his voice weary.

'Or committed murder,' Regan said.

'There was a shot,' Imlach said as Fine frowned. 'From a distance we saw Fran Parker tumble from her horse. She went down like a log.'

'But by the time we got there,' Regan

said, 'he'd managed to throw her across her horse and slip away into the timber.'

'He?'

'Scar-face. Pike Rickman.'

'You go after him?'

'It seemed to me,' Mick Imlach said, 'we'd been like rabid dogs chasin' our tails in tight circles for far too long. We know damn well Rickman's after the cash from the bank robbery. Flint D'Arragon's the only man who knows where that's stashed. Somewhere on the San Pedro seems like a safe bet, but . . . '

'So what Mick figured,' Dave Regan said, 'was why go charging into the woods after Rickman when we already had a damn good idea where he was headed?'

'I still disagree,' Parker said, his face thunderous. 'We had a chance, and on Imlach's say so you two experienced lawmen threw it away. I can't believe you didn't go after Rickman, can't understand why you let him slip away after you saw my daughter gunned down — '

'We heard a shot, saw your daughter fall,' Imlach said. 'The two ain't necessarily connected. Besides, if she's dead there was nothing we could do; if she's alive she'll stay alive longer if we back off.'

'Dead or alive,' John Parker said, 'she's still in his hands, and for that you two must take the blame.'

For a moment there was silence. Then Parker, his eyes on Imlach, said, 'And what about Flint D'Arragon? You've told us he was there one minute, gone the next, but I still don't understand how he slipped away from you — how you could have allowed that to happen.'

'The heat of the moment, the distraction of what looked like your daughter taking a bullet . . . ' Imlach saw the tension in the big man's face and shoulders, the look in the dark eyes that told him the big businessman was way out of his depth, lashing out without thinking at the nearest target. Maybe he *had* made a mistake letting D'Arragon slip away — but already the big businessman had forgotten about questioning the marshal, about the implied accusation, and was lost in his grief.

Without a word, Imlahch went behind the desk, leaned across Jim Fine, slid open a drawer and straightened with a bottle of whiskey in his hand. He found glasses, poured four shots, handed one to the big business-man. The drink was thrown back with as much effect as tepid water. Parker shook his head, glowered into the empty glass.

'Your daughter's Rickman's insurance,' Imlach said reassuringly. 'I don't know what the hell went on out there in the desert, maybe some crazy game he was playing as a warning of what will happen if we push him, but for him to harm your daughter makes no sense. He'll hunt for D'Arragon, force him to reveal where the money's stashed — or make a deal — and when that happens your daughter will be set free.'

'But D'Arragon,' John Parker said, 'is not likely to hang around. He slipped away from you, but how many more chances can he expect? He's a man on the run, with knowledge of a gunny-sack of money he wants all for himself. Why would he come to Redrock? He'll make for the San Pedro, Rickman will do the same, and that leaves us sitting here like — '

'I think he's right,' Jim Fine cut in, his eyes on his boss. 'D'Arragon's got too much to lose to risk showing his face here. He'll make full use of darkness, push on to the river.'

Imlach nodded, pondering on his deputy's words. The way Fine saw it, if they hung around all night in Redrock, by morning D'Arragon could be ten hours ahead of them and racing for the border with the cash in his saddle-bags and Rickman in hot pursuit. The scar-faced man would take Fran Parker with him and, if they made it into Mexico, rescuing the girl would be nigh on impossible. And the money would go with them.

But Mick Imlach remembered Flint D'Arragon positing another disturbing theory.

'Common sense tells me you're right, Jim,' Imlach said, thinking carefully, 'but I'd hate to believe we're going about this entirely the wrong way now because, without knowing it, we've been wrong right from the start.'

'You thinking of that wild story of D'Arragon's?' Regan said.

Imlach shrugged, momentarily feigned indecision, then nodded. 'Right. He's always protested his innocence. And you were listening when he told us the man killed outside the bank was Rickman's brother. That leads to the obvious conclusion that Rickman himself was the man inside the bank. And if that's right, then we've always been wrong in assuming the money's stashed on the San Pedro.'

'If it's not there,' Fine said, 'where the hell is it?'

'Here's one possibility,' Imlach said. 'D'Arragon suggested the bank's cashier — feller called Price, if I remember right — was involved.' He let that thought hang, sink in, and waited with his eyes asking a question of his deputy.

Fine tasted his drink, frowned. 'Vinny Price has been in work every day since the robbery.'

'Wouldn't it look suspicious,' Imlach said, 'if he wasn't?'

'Sure, and of course if he's guilty he'd know that,' Dave Regan said with some irritation. 'But where does all this leave us? First we had D'Arragon and Rickman pushing for the San Pedro where D'Arragon stashed the bank's money. Now we've got Rickman as the guilty man, the bank's cashier involved, the money Christ knows where — and all on the word of the man who was convicted in the first place.'

For a few long moments there was a thoughtful silence. The four men sipped their whiskey absently and without relish and, as each delved deep into his thoughts and looked at possibilities, it became clear to three of them that the only certainty came from the decision made by a court of law. Flint D'Arragon had been found guilty of robbery and murder. To be turned away from that decision because the convicted man came up with ever more complicated reasons to prove his innocence was to fall for the oldest trick in the book.

Watching them, Imlach knew that the pendulum had swung his way.

'All right,' he said, taking a deep, relieved breath. 'We'll grab a bite to eat, an hour's rest, then head for the San Pedro.'

'Back to chasing shadows,' Dave Regan said, and pursed his lips.

'I know where I picked him up, and he'll return there,' Imlach said.

'Someone should watch this end,' John Parker said.

'Jim Fine will stay here, keep his eyes

and ears open — right?' Regan said, and got a nod of agreement from a steely-eyed Imlach. 'I reckon that's the best we can do,' Regan went on, tossing back his drink. He grimaced sourly. 'But I sure as hell get the feeling Rickman and D'Arragon — separately or together — are playing a game we haven't cottoned on to, and I can see us thrashing around out there in the dark and getting no closer to an answer than we are right now.'

'So let's go and do that,' Mick Imlach said, tight-lipped; and, planting his empty glass on the desk, he turned and made for the door.

15

For D'Arragon, walking into the saloon was like stepping back in time to the night when his loose mouth had set a whole train of events in motion and led to his conviction for robbery and murder. It was also a moment of high risk, when the desperate race to clear his name could all come to naught.

On that night, before he rode to the San Pedro, saloonist Jake Creedy had looked deep into his eyes across the narrow width of his bar and would recognize him on sight. Now, D'Arragon was relying on nothing more subtle than a day's growth of stubble, a pulled-down slouch hat and a greasy black vest to hide his identity.

Also, minutes before booking a room at the hotel, he had stolen a shotgun and shells from a hostler who moved like an old man with one foot in boot hill but had eyes as sharp and as wily as the most cunning of foxes. He'd notice the empty space in the rack as soon as he walked back into his dusty office — hell, hadn't D'Arragon snatched a carefully greased Greener and left the old man a couple of rusting Winchesters with broken levers? — and he'd remember the man with the slouch hat and black vest and come a-hunting.

From the frail old man himself, D'Arragon had nothing to fear, but any verbal altercation would attract attention and, once that happened, the game would be over.

Like right now, D'Arragon thought ruefully, drifting to a table away from the lamplight with his drink and watching the old man come slapping in through the batwing doors, his keen eyes already searching the room.

And settling on D'Arragon.

The fat man polishing glasses behind the bar was not Jake Creedy; he had served D'Arragon without a flicker of recognition in his blank black eyes.

Now the old man said something to him, drew no response, picked up his glass of beer and limped towards D'Arragon; sat down at the table without a by-your-leave; took a long, deep draught of the cool drink, Adam's apple bobbing, then cocked his birdlike head and exposed pink gums in a wily grin.

'When news hit town you'd broke loose,' he said, 'I figured you'd be headin' for Redrock.'

'I guess that newfangled telegraph takes away the element of surprise.'

'Ain't no horse that fast, that's for sure,' the old man said. 'And as soon's the stage hit Yuma without you, the wires were hot.'

'If I was smart enough to walk away from Marshal Imlach, don't you think I'd know news would travel fast? So why did you suppose I'd come back here?'

'Because you didn't rob the bank,' the old man said, and D'Arragon paused with his glass halfway to his lips.

He nodded slowly, feeling something surge inside him — that old, familiar rush of hope — looked into bright blue eyes that were dancing with conspiratorial glee, and took his delayed taste of the harsh liquor.

'Judge Blake convicted me, and would argue against you.'

'Hah!'

'It's always difficult to refute the statement of a reliable eye-witness.'

'Vinny Price? Biggest liar in town.'

'He swore on the Bible, in a court of law.'

'Every man has his price.'

'You mean he was paid by somebody — the real bank robber — to testify against me?'

'Nope.'

D'Arragon touched the side of the cool glass to the point of his chin, rubbed his bristles back and forth against it, searched the old man's eyes.

'Then he was pointing the finger at me to protect the money he'd already made . . . from the robbery.'

'You tellin', or askin'?'

'Let's say I'd sort of reached that conclusion — but confirmation would give me a nice warm feeling.'

'Well, you won't get it from me,' the old man said, and took a swill of beer that went down with a faint gargling sound. 'But think about this: Amos Grant's owned that bank for more than twenty-five years, always been about as secretive as a man can get about bank business and the risky incomings and outgoings of bulk cash.' His eyes narrowed to blue slits. 'Yet the bank robbers hit him on a day when his safe was full to bustin', and the only way they'd've knowed that — could possibly have knowed that for certain — is from somebody inside slippin' them the word.'

'So somebody inside,' D'Arragon said with a twisted smile, 'made the bank robbery possible; somebody outside — me — alerted a town's defences and ensured one bank robber died.'

'Ain't no one sheddin' tears over a

dead owlhoot,' the old man said.

'His brother murdered Amos Grant, and walked out of there with his shotgun smoking,' D'Arragon said.

'Vinny Price walked out alive and well, and more than one pair of eyes in Redrock's linked the two and're waitin' for Vinny to hightail when the dust's settled.'

'So other people think the law got the wrong man?'

The old man shrugged. 'Suspicion without proof. Your average citizen keeps his head down, goes about his business.'

'All right, so if Price runs, where will he hightail from, exactly? Where does he live?'

'Got a house tacked right on the edge of town.' The hostler's grin was gap-toothed. 'Raised on stilts, wide verandy. You'd've passed it the night you rode out to the San Pedro, same again when Imlach brung you in.'

'Lives alone?'

'What woman would share her life

with that mean, cantankerous, lyin' old bastard?'

'If a man's rich enough, there'll always be someone willing to pay the price.'

'Right, with all that cash the Plain Janes and widder women'll be linin' up at his front door — but for that to happen he'll need to move a hell of a long ways from Redrock.'

'And I've got to get to him before he does,' Flint D'Arragon said.

The old man drained his glass. D'Arragon finished his drink, took both glasses to the bar and returned with a fresh beer for the hostler. He stood looking down at the old man, thinking about others in town who suspected there'd been a miscarriage of justice, uplifted by the knowledge that people unwilling to act on his behalf were yet behind him in their thoughts; feeling, again and without surprise the exhilarating onset of that 'inevitable surge of hope' that throughout life had been his watchword.

'If you want to confront Vinny Price,' the old man said slowly, 'now's about the best opportunity you're likely to get.'

'Why?'

'Marshal Imlach and the rest rode out. Makin' for the San Pedro, I'd guess, chasin' a bank robber who broke free and led 'em a merry dance before makin' a beeline for his stash.'

'Thanks, old-timer. There is one complication: the man who walked out of that bank with a smoking shotgun is probably ahead of me and could make this riskier than you'll ever know. But I guess it's face him, or face a life on the run . . .'

And with a shrug that sent a clear message to a shrewd old man, Flint D'Arragon walked out into the night.

16

If Flint D'Arragon heard the faint, almost imperceptible report of a gunshot when he was deep in the livery barn's shadows saddling the Hatch & Hodges' horse, it soon slipped his mind as he pondered with intense excitement on what he had learnt and on what lay ahead. Other people were convinced of his innocence. And, maybe half a mile away, the lonely little man upon whom suspicion had settled like a dark cloud sat alone and unsuspecting in his house on the edge of town.

He rode out into the street with his heart uplifted, saw light flooding from the open door of the jail office and guessed that Imlach would have left Deputy Jim Fine behind to hold the fort. Then he swung east and pushed the horse easily towards the edge of the town's lamplight where silence and darkness encroached and in the haunted stillness the skies above were sprinkled with stars.

Buildings thinned. False-fronted premises gave way to scattered houses with parched flowers struggling to bloom in arid front yards and lights glowing softly behind curtained windows. Then the last house loomed, timber walls stripped of paint by the cruel sun, set back off the street with one of those naked side walls facing town and the other looking blindly towards the Arizona wilderness. From behind the house the cashier's horse sensed their presence, nickered faintly.

Rickety steps climbed to a wide front gallery. In the faint breeze a door creaked.

And what John Flint D'Arragon's nostrils detected on those warm currents of air was enough to tighten his stomach.

He rode into the gateless front yard, slipped from the saddle and tethered the horse to a post, climbed the steps with the old hostler's gleaming shotgun in his hand and cocked and his finger brushing the trigger. When he reached it, the front door moved gently: opening inwards, then coming back towards him, moving stiffly on unoiled hinges.

D'Arragon touched the dry wood with his fingers, hesitated, listened, pushed the door open; looked into darkness and remembered the faint echoes of a gunshot as he sniffed the rank smell of cordite and heard a man softly groan.

He found Vinny Price in the big living-room, flat on his back on an old Navajo rug with his blood soaking the coarse wool and his blind eyes staring up into the darkness. Blind because he was dying, almost gone, and it was with haste that D'Arragon let the shotgun clatter to one side as he knelt down and put his face close to the old cashier's and said, 'Who did this to you, Price?'

A breath rasped against his face. Bony fingers were like claws scratching at his arm, a dying man's meaningless spasm. Price's throat rattled. One heel thumped the floor.

'Price, tell me, who did this, who —?'

'Don't ask him,' Mick Imlach said, 'ask me.'

And he came out of the darkness by the big, cold stone fireplace where he had lurked with a six-gun tight in his fist and on his clothing the reek of gunsmoke and suddenly, to Flint D'Arragon, all became clear.

'You,' he said bitterly, and rocked back on his heels before coming erect. 'In it with Rickman, right from the start. Four of you, then Rickman's brother's death cut that down to three — and now there's just two left to split the money.' He looked from the cashier's cooling body to the shotgun on the Navajo rug a short pace away that was yet a yawning, uncrossable gulf; saw the pistol tilt as Redrock's marshal caught that swift glance, eased back the pistol's hammer, and flashed a savage grin that was an open challenge to D'Arragon. Go for it, that grin said.

Go for it, and right here in this room is where it ends.

D'Arragon looked at the white patch on the marshal's scalp, the line of dark stitches, and he said with bitter regret, 'Christ, why didn't I hit you harder?'

And the crooked marshal laughed.

'What was poor Vinny Price?' D'Arragon said. 'The man who made things easy for Rickman inside the bank, the man who was keeping the cash safe here until the dust settled, the man who was sure to end up penniless and dead because what was happening was out of his league and there never was going to be a four-way split?'

'All those things.'

'And what about me? When did I come into it?'

'When you opened your mouth to Jake Creedy,' Imlach said, 'a sucker dropped into my lap.'

'But it all went wrong when I broke loose.'

'A setback. You were a convicted

killer running free.' Imlach gestured lazily with his left hand. 'It was bound to sort itself out, given time.'

'The town hostler . . . '

'Kelly.'

'Less than an hour ago he saw you ride out with Regan and Parker. What happened?'

'Back there on the trail you'd already pointed the finger at Vinny. I told the others I'd drop by, check his story, catch them up later.'

'Another tall story.'

'As it happens, that's exactly what I'm going to do.'

D'Arragon frowned. 'Why? You're here, you've got the money, now you join Rickman and together you ride south to the Mex border.' He tilted his head, saw the sudden anger flare behind the marshal's eyes.

'That was the idea, of course,' Imlach said, 'but Rickman got here first.'

'And now *he's* got the money,' D'Arragon said softly, suddenly understanding. 'You didn't kill Price, did you, that was Rickman?'

'He forced the old feller to tell him where the money was hid, when he'd got what he wanted . . . ' Imlach shrugged.

The pistol had drooped as the marshal's emotions took control and he raged mentally over what might have been. D'Arragon looked again at the shotgun, weighed his chances; backed away and went around the table to the window. The lights of Redrock glowed to his left. In the other direction there was nothing but darkness. Rickman was out there somewhere, with a packed gunny sack and a pretty, dark-haired girl who was now witness to murder and who had a story to tell.

'If Fran Parker talks,' D'Arragon said, 'you're finished.' He swung to face Imlach. 'That's the only reason you've come clean, isn't it?'

'No, it's not. I've come clean because it doesn't matter, if you live to tell the tale nobody will ever believe you. But you're right about Fran Parker. Vinny was alive when I got here, long enough to say a few words. Seems Rickman let slip I was involved from the outset. Now Vinny's dead, but the girl's carrying that secret with her.'

D'Arragon reached for his top pocket, saw the marshal's eyes follow his hand as he found the makings and began fashioning a cigarette. As the match flared D'Arragon blew smoke, rested both his hands on the back of a straight-backed chair and nodded slowly.

'If you didn't come clean because the girl already knows the truth,' D'Arragon said, 'then there can be only one other reason for spilling the beans.' He rocked the chair back on to two legs. 'So this is the way I see it now. You plug me, ride hard after Rickman, tackle him and in the gunfight the girl dies. You also kill Rickman. And so you've done it all. The man who gunned down Vinny Price is dead — me, a convicted killer with a motive. The man who kidnapped and shot John

Parker's daughter is also dead — Pike Rickman. And you've got your hands on the money, but nobody knows that.'

'Neat,' Imlach said, and flashed a grin. Across the table, the pistol lifted, its black muzzle huge.

And Flint D'Arragon brought up the flimsy chair and threw it in a roundhouse sweep at the marshal's grinning face.

17

The flying chair hit hard, the end of one leg driving into Imlach's throat as he pulled the trigger. The chair splintered, wrapping itself around his shoulders. Wildly, he flung it away, brought the six-gun level, pulled the trigger. The slug whistled past D'Arragon's ear. Half blinded by the muzzle flash, ears ringing from the report, he stepped forward and with both hands tipped the table and rolled the top edge hard into the gagging lawman's thighs.

Imlach's boot heel caught in the rug. He went down, roaring his rage. Shielded by the table now lying on its side, D'Arragon dipped low to scoop up the Greener. He came up fast, snapping back the hammers, swung the shotgun around — and Imlach had gone.

The six-gun flashed again, the second shot coming from the corner of the stone fireplace. This time D'Arragon felt a tremendous blow in his left arm. He spun away, driven by the power of the bullet striking muscle, felt his knees turn to water, his fingers slacken on the shotgun as a third shot instantly followed that crippling second. This one howled harmlessly off through the open front door. Fighting the mist of weakness drifting before his eyes, D'Arragon dropped behind the table, blinking hard. Across the room there was a blur of movement, dancing sideways. He brought the shotgun up, slammed it on the table's edge, pulled the trigger. The roar of the blast was accompanied by the rattle of buckshot hitting the back wall, the tinkle of shattering glass.

The room was brightly illuminated, as if by a flash of lightning.

In that brief moment of dazzling light, D'Arragon saw the marshal twisting away into the chimney alcove.

Fumbling, he swiftly brought the shotgun up again, the muzzle hunting that darting shape. Then common sense restrained him and he lifted his twitching finger off the trigger: the Greener was double-barrelled, he'd fired one shot and if this one missed he was unarmed and done for — and Imlach would know that.

And then the wily marshal proved that he was also astute enough to realize that if D'Arragon held back that single powerful shot, there would come a moment when the six-gun was empty, the roles would be reversed and he would be at the other man's mercy. Knowing that time was running out, aware that D'Arragon would nurse that last shell and hold his fire, the marshal went across the room at an unhurried lope and, tucked into a tight ball, leaped through the shattered rear window.

★   ★   ★

A pulse like a hissing drum beat. The fading clatter of hoofs. The soft, liquid drip of blood.

Mere moments had passed, but Flint D'Arragon was down on one knee listening to Mick Imlach make his escape as strength leaked out of his torn arm and the dark room in which Vinny Price lay dead lurched sickeningly.

He clenched his jaw, ripped the bandanna from around his neck and used fingers and teeth to pull it tight around his blood-soaked upper arm; closed his eyes, braced himself; took several deep, shuddering breaths; swallowed hard and opened his eyes to gaze blearily at a steadier room.

And think hard.

Dave Regan and John Parker were making for the San Pedro. Pike Rickman had the money and was almost certainly riding hard for the Mexican border — but he was in the middle, caught between Regan and Parker, and the crooked lawman he had double-crossed. Under normal circumstances, Rickman wouldn't stand a chance.

But the scar-faced killer had his hole card: he had Fran Parker.

D'Arragon stood up, swayed as nausea returned, steadied himself by bracing his knees against the heavy, fallen table until the giddiness passed. And, as he fought against the waves of weakness that threatened to overwhelm him, so he cursed bitterly under his breath. Time was his enemy. Outside, the hoof-beats had faded into silence. For every second he stood there, sick and helpless, Imlach drew further away from him and closer to a bloody showdown with Regan and Parker. And while Rickman held a hole card that had long been turned face up and so lost some of its shock value, Mick Imlach had a terrible and potentially fatal advantage over his two former colleagues, Parker and Regan: he was one of them; they trusted him, and they would be blind to his treachery.

Move, damn you!

Cursing himself for a weak, spineless, indecisive, yellow-bellied, son of a bitch, Flint D'Arragon pushed away from the table and stumbled out of that room of death. He went down the steps at a tumbling run, falling heavily to his knees in the packed earth of the yard and again driving himself up and on with a raging torrent of curses. He dragged himself into the saddle, teeth bared in a grinning rictus of agony, kicked the startled horse into a walk, then a run, and swung away from Vinny Price's house at a fast gallop with the lights of Redrock at his back and the prospect of savage gunplay somewhere ahead in the darkness.

And he had ridden a full mile at that furious, reckless pace when he was hit by the realization that he had shells in his saddle-bag but the shotgun that was his only weapon lay alongside a dead man on a bloodstained Navajo rug.

★ ★ ★

The cloud had slipped away from the high full moon and deep waters were a glittering ribbon snaking south as Regan and Parker reined in under silver-grey cottonwoods fringing an ox-bow on the San Pedro river.

John Parker's scepticism had come back with a vengeance.

'You still think this is a good idea?'

'Mick Imlach was absolutely sure: this is the spot where he arrested D'Arragon; he had no cash on him when he was picked up, so it has to be stashed here. If it's here, then — '

'If.' Parker spat his disdain into the dust. 'What if the cashier was in on it, the cash left in his safekeeping?'

'That's why Mick told us ride on while he goes to Price's house, talks to the man.'

'If the money is there, then what we're doing is continuing a wild-goose chase,' Parker said bitterly. 'Or maybe we are on the right track, but too late, Rickman's already got together with D'Arragon and they've dug up the money and lit out for the border.'

'Maybe. We've been running around in circles ever since Flint D'Arragon stopped that stage and rode away into the desert. He's led us a dance, first one way, then another, with him and Rickman behind us then in front of us and now Christ knows where. So all we can do is wait, and hope we've got something right for a change. If they've been and gone' — Regan shrugged — 'well, we'll know soon enough and somewhere between here and the border they'll set your daughter free. Then it'll be up to the Rurales to hunt down D'Arragon and Rickman, and for all the good that'll do we might as well kiss them and the money goodbye and — '

'Riders coming!'

The two men eased their horses back into the trees, rustling into the dappled shade. On the still night air the hoofbeats swiftly swelled from a distant whisper to an insistent pounding as the approaching riders pushed south, and

Regan, listening hard, swore harshly.

'I make two of them.'

'So not Imlach.'

'Let's pray it's Rickman and D'Arragon.'

'Yeah, and if Fran's already free then those two bastards are going to pay for what they've done.'

But Regan was no longer listening. Mick Imlach had been precise in his directions, and Regan knew he'd brought Parker to the right location on the San Pedro. But the two riders, now almost upon them, were not slackening their pace. If they were after the stashed money then Regan would have expected them to slow, swing in off the wide, open trail and make for the stand of cottonwoods clearly visible in the bright moonlight. Instead . . .

'Something's wrong.'

But Parker had already sensed that something was amiss and, six-gun out and cocked, was moving his horse out of the trees into cold moonlight and across the coarse grass to the trail to intercept the riders. Even as he did so, they came around a low rise and hammered towards him, riding close together — impossibly close — and as realization hit the watching Regan, he spurred his horse out of the trees and yelled a warning.

'It's Rickman and your daughter; hold your fire, John!'

Parker had moved fast, and was already pulling his horse to a halt across the trail. And the thunder of hoofs drowned Regan's words. As the Yuma sheriff watched in horror, John Parker bared his teeth in a snarl and loosed a wild shot at the riders thundering down on him.

'No!' Regan roared.

Split seconds had passed. The sound of the shot was still a lingering echo. But Regan's shout was too late.

This time, Parker heard him, and his eyes glinted in the moonlight as he looked back to see what was wrong. But in front of him, all was chaos. The shot had winged Fran Parker: the businessman had shot his own daughter. In a replay of what had been enacted before them on the Yuma trail, the girl swayed on the bare back of the Hatch & Hodges' horse, and appeared about to fall. But the horse had other ideas. At the crack of the shot its ears had flattened and, without bidding from the girl, it slowed abruptly from full gallop to a skidding halt with all four legs braced. Dust boiled. The horse squealed in fright. Fran Parker, about to fall backwards, was flung bodily forward to cling on desperately with her arms wrapped around the animal's neck — and as the lead rope linking her to Pike Rickman snapped taut, it broke.

Suddenly, she was free.

The horse, still skittish and for a long time frustrated by the annoying rope restricting its movements, felt the sudden lightness, lifted its head and turned to trot briskly towards the sullen metallic glint of the river.

It was as if the world stood still.

Pike Rickman had heard the shot and felt the rope snap, and now reined in hard. John Parker was whitefaced, smoking six-gun tilted as Regan's first words finally registered and he gazed in frozen horror at the girl slumped on the horse that was already splashing into the waters of the San Pedro. Dave Regan had also come to a halt. In bright moonlight, tragedy had locked the three men in a stark tableau where dust and the smoke from a single gunshot were slowly settling.

That moment couldn't be sustained, couldn't last.

The scar-faced Pike Rickman was the first to move.

His six-gun came out and up in a fast draw that was followed instantly by a blinding flash, the bark of the shot. The bullet hit home with a meaty thump. Regan's horse grunted, and collapsed. It went down in a heap, trapping Regan's right leg, pinning him to the hard ground.

The shot broke through Parker's

daze. With a cry of horror he kicked his horse towards the river. And in the river, away from the steep bank where water danced white under the flashing hoofs of Fran Parker's horse, the second shot continued its deadly work: at the sharp crack that was intensified by the night silence the already startled horse rolled its eyes, leaped forward into deep water, tried to rear as the river bottom went from under it and threw the wounded girl clear. Legs and arms flailing, she fell backwards, hit the water flat and went under.

At the same moment, Pike Rickman loosed three more rapid shots. Parker's running horse went down, slid, lay still. Parker, thrown clear, tried to rise then collapsed with a groan, clutching his thigh.

And pinned under his horse, fighting to drag his leg free or at the very least get a hand to his six-gun, Dave Regan watched helplessly as Pike Rickman flashed a savage grin and rode off into the night.

Flint D'Arragon heard the shots when he was a full half-mile away from the ox-bow where he had camped. At once he put spurs to his horse, gritting his teeth as the pounding and jolting of the hard ride increased and pain knifed through his arm.

He caught the tang of gunsmoke as he rounded the low rise and the cottonwoods loomed; came upon a scene of chaos where a man was pinned to the ground by his mount, another lay groaning some yards away from a second dead horse, and a third horse with its ears flattened to its head came thrashing up out of the boiling white waters of the San Pedro.

A Hatch & Hodges' horse.

But where was Fran Parker?

His horse still pulling to a halt, D'Arragon tumbled from the saddle and hit the ground at a stumbling run.

'In the water!'

The frantic yell came from big John

187

Parker, half sitting now, struggling to rise with his right leg blood-soaked. Then he recognized the newcomer. With a snarl he reached for his pistol, realized he'd lost it in the fall, roared his impotent fury to the night skies.

Dave Regan, still struggling to free himself, was more clear-headed.

'John fired wild, winged the girl,' he called to D'Arragon. 'Her horse threw her, she's in the river,' he said crisply.

But D'Arragon's searching eyes had already picked out the pale white oval of the girl's face as she surfaced, seen her sluggish movements as she floated then sank, and already he was past the impotently fuming Parker and sliding down the bank.

The cold water took his breath away, tore his stiffening shirt sleeve from the congealing blood and a hot wave of pain momentarily blurred his vision. Then he was chest deep and wading. He reached the floundering, spluttering girl, took a handful of cotton top and with his good arm dragged her to his chest and started back. A patch of soft sand underfoot ducked him, threatened to drag him all the way down, then gave way to stony ground and he thrust himself up, choking. The girl's arm settled around his neck, soft and clinging, her clear dark eyes wide open and watching him. He forced a grin, clamped his mouth shut as icy water slapped his face. Then he was at the bank, gasping, leaning against the slope of wet grass, unable to move. Her arm slid from around his neck. He saw the dark blood on her shoulder as she reached for his hand, held it with a fierce grip. Together they struggled against the sucking weight of the water, clawed their way up the bank; collapsed panting on the crisp, dry grass.

'And here's where it ends,' John Parker said.

Still down, he'd nevertheless found and picked up his dusty pistol. It was cocked, levelled at Flint D'Arragon.

'Move away from her; can't you see she's hurt bad?'

'A flesh wound, Pa,' Fran Parker said, and clung to D'Arragon's hand. 'And you're pointing your gun at the wrong man, D'Arragon robbed no bank, committed no murder.'

'Ha!' Parker's gaze was cynical. 'He tell you that — and you believe him?'

'A man called Vinny Price convinced me, when he complained bitterly with his dying breath as the man who'd shot him in cold blood — Pike Rickman — dragged a gunny-sack stuffed with money from under his bed.'

And then a second voice spoke up.

'Do as he says, D'Arragon. Move away.'

Dave Regan had at last dragged his leg from under the dead horse, squirmed around and reached his six-gun. It was out, pointing nowhere in particular but nevertheless there to back up the deadly intent that glinted in the Yuma sheriff's narrowed eyes.

'Imlach's got other things on his mind,' D'Arragon said, gently disengaging the girl's hand and standing up. 'He was in on the robbery from the start, along with Price and the Rickman brothers.'

Regan looked at him intently, his face unreadable. 'That's not the way it looks,' he said, climbing awkwardly to his feet. 'In front of me I see a convicted man with a bullet-torn arm, turning up in the middle of the night at the place he stashed the Redrock bank's money.'

'Just hold on a minute,' John Parker said. There was weakness in his voice, and the hand clasping his thigh was dark with blood. 'I don't know about Imlach's involvement — I find that very hard to swallow — but my daughter says she heard a dying man say D'Arragon's innocent, and that bears thinking about.'

'But while we waste time thinking and jawing,' D'Arragon said, 'Rickman is racing for the border with the cash, Imlach somewhere out there but surely not too far behind.'

For a moment there was silence

broken only by the big businessman's harsh breathing, the soft whisper of the river. Then Regan grunted, pouched his pistol and began unbuckling his gun-belt.

'Who plugged you?'

'Imlach.'

'Where? In Price's house?'

'I told you some time back I wanted to talk to the cashier. He was dead when I got there, Imlach lurking in the shadows. He threw down on me, there was some shooting — '

'Sure there was. Imlach was there to talk to Price, when you walked in it was his duty to arrest you.'

'Maybe, but what he did do was admit he was involved; that Rickman had taken cash that was supposed to be shared out.'

'Your word against his, if it ever comes up.' Regan shook his head, clearly puzzled. 'And so Imlach admitted his guilt, then let you get away?'

'Nope. There was a kind of impasse and he jumped out the window.'

'I guess his mind was on the money?'

On Regan's face there was the clear knowledge that the question he had posed could be taken two ways, and D'Arragon smiled thinly in acknowledgement. He walked over, took the gunbelt from Regan, buckled it around his waist. The marshal was down again, massaging his twisted leg. Fran Parker had crossed to her father and was attending to his wound, the big man now flat on his back and tight-lipped with pain.

'Looking at the three of you I'd say there's not much you can do to help yourselves,' D'Arragon said to Regan. 'But if things turn out right and I come back this way, I should have two spare horses.'

'*When* you come back this way,' Regan said, 'I'll get this mess sorted out one way or another. And you will come back,' he added, straightfaced, 'if all that money that's on Imlach's mind doesn't go to your head, and turn it.'

D'Arragon looked into his eyes, saw

something there that was immensely reassuring, nodded his thanks for that unvoiced confidence and trust and wheeled away to walk swiftly to his horse.

The last words he heard as he rode away from the cottonwoods were Fran Parker's almost inaudible, 'Take care, D'Arragon.'

Then he was away and running, the pain of his arm a nagging ache that paled into insignificance when compared to the daunting task that lay ahead.

18

He had a bullet-holed arm that was stiffening and giving him seven kinds of hell, rode a weary Hatch & Hodges' horse and carried a borrowed six-gun and, ahead of him, two desperate men were riding a collision course to a violent confrontation over their right to a heap of stolen money. But both men, Flint D'Arragon knew, would agree to delay that deadly duel if he ran them down, for each man had his own special reasons for wanting him dead.

Pike Rickman considered D'Arragon's loose mouth to be the reason behind his brother's death; Mick Imlach had figured shrewdly that if another man was convicted of the crime he'd committed, he was not only rich, but safe.

Yet those reasons to commit cold-blooded murder were as nothing to the torment that was driving Flint D'Arragon towards what he knew was justified retribution. He had been snatched at gunpoint from his campsite on the San Pedro, tried and convicted of robbery and murder, then transported across the desert towards the state penitentiary where he would be incarcerated. Now he had the opportunity to convince good men, honest men, of his innocence. To do it, he had to best Rickman and Imlach; to do it to ensure his conviction was quashed — and in a way that would give him complete satisfaction — he had to take back one or both of those men, alive, to spill his tale to Dave Regan.

A tall order.

As he pushed hard across cruelly rugged terrain lighted by a now waning moon, the hope that had blossomed when he looked into Dave Regan's eyes was struggling to stay alive. Imlach had a good start, Rickman was even further ahead. The odds were stacked against him riding either of them down, and if they did make the border and cross into Mexico, he was finished. And so he pushed on, blanking his mind to the pain of his wound, always squinting ahead for that tell-tale plume of dust that would indicate the position of one of the fleeing men; always aware that there were four points to a compass, and the men he was following blind could have chosen to ride any one of them.

And then he saw it, and held his breath.

Not a plume of dust, but the drifting white smoke from a camp-fire; beneath it as he drew near and cautiously, stealthily slowed the lathered horse, the bright flicker of flame. Horses, tethered against stunted trees. And two men, one standing, pacing, one crouched over a fire built in the shelter between the trees and an outcrop of rock.

Easy now, D'Arragon thought, and felt his chest tighten with apprehension, felt the hope that had been like a dying ember suddenly flare hotly into life.

That's Imlach pacing, Rickman by the fire. They're arguing, the scar-faced man smug because the money's in his saddle-bags, the crooked lawman fuming, first because he's a robber robbed, second because the wily outlaw is trying to talk his way out of trouble and hasn't given him an opening: Imlach wants the money, but he knows damn well it's no use to him dead.

As D'Arragon drew near, riding a wide loop so that the stand of stunted trees was always between him and the two men, their voices drifted to him and he knew he'd figured it right. Imlach's voice was raised, edgy, Rickman's so cool it would be driving the lawman into a rage. Something had to break — and D'Arragon had to decide: did he wait for the explosion when Mick Imlach's patience snapped, or did he pounce on them out of the night and hope that shock would make his limited firepower overwhelming?

Closer, ever closer. Leaning painfully from the saddle, D'Arragon squinted at stony ground lit by weak moonlight and picked a snaking, careful path over the dust that was deposited thickly between the thrusting rocks, a route that deadened all sound from the horse's ringing iron shoes. The merest clink would betray him. He listened to the disembodied voices, rising, falling, held his breath until his chest ached; came up on the gnarled trees like a ghost and slid from the saddle.

And grunted as his left arm caught and dragged on the saddle and pain shot from fingertips to shoulder and weakness forced him to his knees and, beneath him, dead branches screamed a snapping, crackling warning.

The startled horse backed off, crashing noisily through low branches, then a metal shoe slipped ringingly on half-buried stone and the horse slid on slick dead leaves, turned and bolted.

Sudden, ominous silence.

Then an explosion of violence as the rawboned Rickman came up from the fire with his hand stabbing for his holster and Imlach spun, drew and fired in one smooth movement and a bullet hummed wickedly close to D'Arragon's ear.

Already down, he rolled for his life. A second bullet followed the first, snicking through the branches. A third probed for him and stripped sharp splinters from a flat rock before whining into the distance.

Tight-lipped, in agony, D'Arragon lay still.

'Hold your fire,' Rickman told Imlach. Six-gun still pouched he began walking towards the timber, drew level with the marshal, then glanced at the other man's pistol, realized the position he would put himself in — and stopped.

'Only one man would sneak up on us like that,' Imlach said, and laughed. 'D'Arragon's in that scrub. You go after him, I'll cover you.'

'Yeah,' Rickman said cynically, 'you'd like that, wouldn't you?'

'Would solve a couple of pressing

problems,' Imlach said.

'Yours, not mine. I've got a better idea: let's set and wait. Without a horse he's going nowhere. And if you winged him like you said . . . '

'Oh, he's bleeding like a stuck pig.'

'Then he's got a choice,' Rickman said, and now his voice was mocking, purposely pitched high so D'Arragon would hear clearly. 'He stays where he is and bleeds to death like that stuck pig you mentioned, or he comes out to face us — '

'And dies like a man,' Imlach finished for him, and now they were both laughing, the fire flickering at their backs and wan light from the moon casting deep shadows in the hollows of brows and cheekbones and transforming both men's faces into masks of evil.

Exactly what he'd expected, D'Arragon thought. A truce, until he was finished, when they would settle ownership of the bank's money in a deadly gunfight waged over his dead, bleeding body.

But ignoring his desperate position,

ignoring the pain, inside his breast there still flared that bright beacon of hope. He had come this far, had got a tacit acceptance of his innocence from Dave Regan, and he'd told the Yuma sheriff that, if he returned, he would bring back with him two spare horses. And he would do that. He would do it not by lying down and bleeding to death, nor by walking out and dying like a man. He would do it the obvious way, the way two men arrogantly supposing him to be exhausted, bloodied and beaten had completely ignored.

From low down, firing through the scrub without exposing himself or changing his position, Flint D'Arragon took the fight to his enemies as he cut down Pike Rickman with a single aimed shot from Regan's .45 and swiftly switched his aim to the marshal.

But Imlach was fast.

Rickman went down, roaring and clutching his shoulder, and Imlach was gone, leaping cat-like behind the rocky outcrop, snapping a shot at D'Arragon as he went then dropping out of sight. He was gone as D'Arragon's second, much wilder shot raised a shower of sparks, chipped splinters of rock and howled into the night skies.

Now D'Arragon exploited his sudden advantage. Pushing the raging fire of his wounded arm into the background, he sprang to his feet and burst through the scrub to confront Rickman. The man was still wicked and dangerous. He had dropped heavily on to one knee, teeth bared in a snarl, bloodstained fingers clutching his shoulder. He heard the crackle of the scrub, saw D'Arragon leap out of the bushes, executed a lightning fast draw and cocked the six-gun as it came up.

Desperate to get in first, D'Arragon fired twice. The first slug thumped into the ground a yard in front of the outlaw, kicking dust into his eyes; lank blond hair lifted as if picked up by an errant breeze as D'Arragon's second bullet whistled close and nicked the scarred man's ear. Rickman roared, instinctively snapped his head aside, got a shot off. But he was blinking his burning eyes, off balance and hasty. The slug hissed low, hit D'Arragon's boot heel, snapped it, twisted his leg and brought him down. And Rickman's second shot, which would this time have been on target, cut the air where D'Arragon had been standing.

In agony, shooting from the ground where he had been dumped hard, D'Arragon fired twice more. Rickman took both slugs in his body, rocked backwards, managed a sneer despite the terrible effect of the two bullets and struggled to hold his six-gun level. Once more D'Arragon pulled the trigger — and was shocked to hear a metallic click as the hammer fell on an empty chamber.

On both knees, slammed back on to his heels and his shirt front a glistening mess of blood, Pike Rickman struggled to centre his pistol on the helpless D'Arragon's chest. The rawboned outlaw flashed a terrible grin as he succeeded; his knuckle began whitening on the trigger.

The wait for the blast of the shot was marked by a terrible silence. The night was electric with menace, strung wire-taut with unbearable tension.

D'Arragon had spare shells in the loops on Regan's gunbelt but he had run out of time, and with a bloodied and useless left arm he couldn't reach them or reload. The click of his empty six-gun had been loud, screaming a clear message that announced his helplessness and defeat. Horribly exposed in open moonlight and clutching an empty pistol, he caught the flash of movement as Mick Imlach rose brazenly from behind the rock outcrop, saw the pistol glittering in the marshal's fist, waited for the twin muzzle flashes and the shuddering impact of shells from both men that would snuff out the blaze of hope burning within him and signify the end of his heroic fight for justice and freedom.

Then the glittering, malevolent light

in Pike Rickman's eyes filmed over, dulled, winked out. The pistol he was holding drooped, fell from his hand. The big outlaw toppled sideways, and the air rattled horribly in his throat as he took his last breath, and died.

D'Arragon looked hungrily at the big man's pistol. It lay ten feet away. By D'Arragon's count, there were at least two shells in its cylinder. He drew a breath, whipped his good right arm back and in a fast overhand throw hurled his empty six-gun at Mick Imlach. In the same movement he dived for Rickman's pistol, in a red haze of pain stretched for it, scrabbled for it, found his fingers inches short and dug in his toes and wriggled, wriggled —

And, through the haze, heard the steely clatter of his pistol as it bounced uselessly off the outcrop, heard the mockery in the marshal's voice as he laughed softly. Then a pistol cracked. Hot lead raked across the knuckles of his frantically reaching hand. A second shot spanged against the pistol that was inches from his hand and sent it leaping and bounding like a live thing into the scrub.

★　★　★

'Your word against mine,' Imlach said.

They were hunkered by the fire. Close to them, the dead Rickman was belly-down over his saddle, the flickering light glinting on the lank, dangling blond hair.

'The money's yours,' D'Arragon said hoarsely. 'Take it and run, that's what you've worked for.' And he spat his disgust into the flames.

'A man gets in real deep he sees things in a different light,' Imlach said. 'Let me tell you, a close association with a man like Pike Rickman is an eye-opener to a decent man. Strutting around with pockets stuffed with money has its attractions, but a man with my background and prospects begins asking himself if he wants that kind of life, with men of that breed.'

'Maybe you're in *too* deep to go back, spilled too many secrets to talk your way back into favour.'

'We'll see. I'm still wearing a badge. All those involved in the robbery who might speak against me are dead — '

'Fran Parker?'

'I'm sure, in the heat of the moment, she misheard a dying man,' Imlach said with disconcerting logic. 'Regan will understand that; or maybe she heard right, but the words Price uttered with his dying breath were lies to get even with a strict town marshal he'd never cottoned to . . . ' Imlach shrugged. 'That leaves you and, as I said, it puts the word of a convicted killer against that of a respected town marshal.'

No contest!

He'd looked at D'Arragon's bullet-holed arm, strapped it with strips torn from Rickman's shirt, and there was some relief. But relief from pain, D'Arragon mused despairingly, was small comfort when once again he faced a lifetime in Yuma penitentiary — if Imlach's story was believed.

And why shouldn't it be? Rickman's brother had died in the dust outside the Redrock bank. Pike Rickman had killed Price. And now Rickman himself was dead and Imlach had the outlaw's body belly-down, the stolen money in the outlaw's saddle-bags, and the fourth member of the gang was again his prisoner — John Flint D'Arragon.

In that, the blackest of moments, for Flint D'Arragon the dying flame of hope that had never let him down was just a distant, sputtering memory.

★ ★ ★

They rode down towards the San Pedro out of a moonless night with dawn only hours away, and once again D'Arragon was looking ahead to the flickering light of a camp-fire where figures silhouetted against dancing flames awaited his arrival. They waited not with guns, but with high expectations. Well, they'd get a story and an outcome sure enough, D'Arragon thought bitterly, but not the one he'd planned.

He had vowed to return with two spare horses. Instead, he rode back as a prisoner, Dave Regan's and Pike Rickman's gunbelts hanging from Mick Imlach's saddle-horn, the dead Pike Rickman a bloody, gruesome bulk on the third horse. And the sad fact was that, to Regan or the others, D'Arragon's plight mattered not a jot. Fran Parker was safe, they had the bank's money, and now they had the man who had sweet-talked his way towards innocence and been proved a liar.

John Parker was dozing close to the fire's warmth, his head on a saddle, wounded leg outstretched. Fran Parker's eyes where huge as she stood up to greet them. Regan's face was impassive, his eyes unreadable as he watched the riders approach, watched them swing down on the fringe of the nearby cottonwoods and loose-tie the horses.

'Not quite what I expected,' he said, as Imlach and D'Arragon approached the fire. He could have been talking to either of the men, but he was looking at D'Arragon, a question in his eyes.

'Marshal Imlach's got a story to tell,' D'Arragon said.

'No story,' Imlach said, hunkering down by the fire. 'The truth, and that hasn't changed. D'Arragon, Price and the Rickman brothers planned a bank robbery. Three of them're dead, the money's been recovered, the fourth man will go to jail.'

'I've no argument with that,' Dave Regan said.

Imlach looked up quickly. 'So it's over. And turned out well.'

'Right,' Regan said. 'We're short of horses, but once we get that sorted out — who's riding double, and so forth — we'll head for town.'

'The fourth man can ride with his dead sidekick,' John Parker said huskily.

'That sounds like poetic justice, John,' Regan said approvingly. 'Partners in crime, together again on the owlhoot — but before you climb up behind Rickman, Mick, unbuckle your gunbelt and step away from it.'

In the sudden, aching silence, unheard, unseen, D'Arragon eased away from the fire. Back from the flames, the cool air touched his face, refreshed him. He backed away, one step, then another; heard the soft snuffling of the horse that was now but two or three steps behind him as Imlach began his protests.

'Me? My gunbelt? What the hell are you talking about, Dave?'

'I told you I had no argument. The fourth man *will* go to jail. That's you, Mick.'

'Now just hold on a minute — !'

'No, you listen. Fran Parker heard Vinny Price brand you as guilty with his dying breath — '

'Maybe she heard right, but it was a damned lie, the old fool always hated me.'

'He was telling the truth. You went to

his house for the money, but Rickman beat you to it. And then you slipped up. You knew Flint D'Arragon was going to talk to the cashier. He caught you there, there was gunplay, and you foolishly admitted your involvement in the robbery.'

'A convicted killer,' Imlach said, and laughed harshly. 'His word against mine, Dave — and he's lying to save his skin.'

'No,' Dave Regan said. 'He's not.'

'You slipped up right at the beginning,' Fran Parker said. 'We've had nothing to do but wait here by the river, so we've been discussing it — and it all adds up.'

'Remember back in the Yuma office?' Regan said. 'Old Tom Gaines asked you about the big feller with blond hair and a scarred face. Asked you his name.'

'Pike Rickman.' Imlach nodded, but suddenly there was the sheen of sweat on his face and he took a step back from the fire.'

'That's right,' Regan said, his eyes

never leaving the other man's face. 'When we were leaving, Tom spoke to me, on the stairs. Rickman didn't introduce himself at the stage, you *couldn't* have known his name — '

'Maybe I'd seen his name somewhere, on a didger — '

'Tom asked you that, too; you denied knowing or ever hearing of the man.'

'So I was wrong. You can't connect me to the robbery on that flimsy evidence.'

'Some kind of signal passed between you and Rickman as he rode off. Tom saw that, too.'

'Godammit, the old fool's lying!'

'No!' Regan's voice cracked like a whip. 'I've known that old-timer for years, he doesn't know how to lie.' He paused, took a breath, calmed himself. 'All right, no, I can't connect you on Tom's word alone. But taken alongside Price's dying utterance which Fran Parker heard, taken alongside your admission of guilt to Flint D'Arragon — which I believe happened — then with Tom's sworn testimony and all the rest taken into account I reckon I've got the makings of a case against you.' His grin was suddenly wide, wicked and challenging. 'And d'you know what, Imlach? I don't think you'll risk facing — '

Mick Imlach went for his gun.

He shocked the unarmed Regan with his speed, shocked the girl who stood frozen and helpless; shocked the armed John Parker who was supine, weak, and incapable of reacting with any speed.

But D'Arragon was ready.

As the argument built to a climax, he had taken the two backward steps necessary to bring him up against Imlach's horse. He heard the final explosive words that he knew would drive Imlach to action — 'I don't think you'll risk facing' — and he reached up to the gunbelt hanging from the saddlehorn and slipped Pike Rickman's pistol from the holster.

'Drop it, Imlach!'

Imlach spun. His teeth were bared in

a snarl of fury. The six-gun was levelled, his finger on the trigger, his eyes blazing.

Coolly, without hesitation, D'Arragon shot him through the heart.

The Redrock marshal went down like an empty sack, crumpling slackly.

'I guess,' Dave Regan said softly, 'that ties up the last loose end.'

'To your satisfaction?'

'You heard what I said. Tom Gaines suspected Imlach from the start, and he's a shrewd no-nonsense, blunt-talking feller. I've been watching Imlach since we rode out of Yuma.'

'And now?'

'It gives me considerable pleasure to say this: you're a free man, D'Arragon.'

And as John Flint D'Arragon took the Yuma sheriff's proffered hand, and shook it, he was looking beyond the lawman to the dark-haired girl he had spoken to only briefly over another camp-fire in very different circumstances.

They had a lot to catch up on, and all the free time in the world.

We do hope that you have enjoyed reading this large print book.

Did you know that all of our titles are available for purchase?

We publish a wide range of high quality large print books including:
Romances, Mysteries, Classics
General Fiction
Non Fiction and Westerns

Special interest titles available in large print are:
The Little Oxford Dictionary
Music Book, Song Book
Hymn Book, Service Book

Also available from us courtesy of Oxford University Press:
Young Readers' Dictionary
(large print edition)
Young Readers' Thesaurus
(large print edition)

For further information or a free brochure, please contact us at:
Ulverscroft Large Print Books Ltd.,
The Green, Bradgate Road, Anstey,
Leicester, LE7 7FU, England.
Tel: (00 44) **0116 236 4325**
Fax: (00 44) **0116 234 0205**

Other titles in the
Linford Western Library:

WEST OF EDEN

Mike Stall

Marshal Jack Adams was tired of people shooting at him. So when the kid came into town sporting a two-gun rig and out to make his reputation — at Adams' expense — it was time to turn in his star and buy that horse ranch he'd dreamed about in the Eden Valley. It looked peaceful, but the valley was on the verge of a range-war and there was only one man to stop it. So Adams pinned on a star again and started shooting back — with a vengeance!